Out of the Shadows

Tales to Frighten the Mind
and Rattle the Spine

by

Patrick James Ryan

BLACK BED
SHEET

Out of the Shadows
A Black Bed Sheet/Diverse Media Book
July 2019

Copyright © 2019 by Patrick James Ryan
All rights reserved.

Cover and art by Nicholas Grabowsky
Copyright © 2019 by Black Bed Sheet Books.

The selections in this book are works of fiction. Names, characters, places and incidents either are the product of the author's imagination or are used fictitiously, and any resemblance to actual persons, living or dead, events, or locales is entirely coincidental.

No part of this book may be reproduced, stored in a retrieval system, or transmitted by any means, electronic, mechanical, photocopying, recording, or otherwise, without written permission from the author.

ISBN-10: 1-946874-15-9
ISBN-13: 978-1-946874-15-3

Out of the Shadows

A Black Bed Sheet/Diverse Media Book
Antelope, CA

Also by Patrick James Ryan

Blood Verse

The Night It Got Out

Blood Prose

The Maggots Underneath the Porch

Contents:

Over the Edge 1
Spider 23
Puzzles 64
The Lonely Deaths of
Booker and Chance 75
The Jupiter
Chronicles 92
Hitchin' a Ride 102
The Bunker 116
The Ripper
Returns 151
Ma's Eats 183
Author's Notes 213

✝

This book is dedicated to the loving
memory of Jim and Cathy Birch

Out of the Shadows

Patrick James Ryan

Over the Edge

Gene Reynolds failed to notice the four unsavory young men walk in the diner, or he just might have gotten up from the corner booth and left. The pervasive stress of life had consumed all thought and eclipsed self-awareness, making Gene a bundle of nerves for the last several months. Struggling with significant marital strife from an overbearing wife, feeling undervalued and unappreciated at work, and battling a troubling psychological demon, Gene felt constantly threatened enough to go over the edge.

Reserved and demure at an early age, Gene had evolved into the prototype of someone who could walk into a room full of people and walk out without ever being noticed. A few hairs less than six feet, slightly built, brown hair and brown eyes, his appearance and demeanor were completely forgettable.

Overly vigilante and self-conscious about his tendency to succumb to anxiety and stress, Gene worked hard to cultivate the level of discipline required to control the collective angst in normal circumstances. However, in times of extreme pressure and stress, he sometimes yielded to external triggers when they mounted to a point where he could no longer bear them, forcing him over the edge, a euphemism he coined for the extreme anxiety episodes. When these troubling incidents occurred,

Gene's ability to function rationally and control his emotions was severely compromised. The anxiety paralyzed him.

Since first acquiring this condition about four months ago, Gene experienced two panic attack episodes of going over the edge. One at home, triggered by a particularly bad argument with his denigrating wife, resulting in the destruction of some lamps and wall hangings in the basement in anger, when she locked him in down there. The other on the way home from a business trip, when some young punk cut him off on the highway, landing his humble Ford Prius in a muddy ditch with no way out. He awakened three miles away on a family farm, sweaty and muddy, having no idea how – or for how long – he had been there, and had a horrible time getting assistance to recover the mud caked vehicle out of the ditch.

Gene left the modest, paint-peeling Cape Cod house around 6:40 PM, fleeing from yet another spousal assault about money, fraught in verbal vitriol, an increasingly common event from the selfish bitch he lived with. Seeking solace in the quiet corner booth at Nancy's Diner, Gene tried valiantly to control his anxiety and get it to dissipate. His mind was miles away as he took a generous mouthful of Nancy's famous Key Lime Pie, when the four recently escaped convicts from Mansfield Juvenile Correctional Facility descended on the diner.

***

Waitress Shelly Cox knew the four men were trouble the moment they strolled into the diner, reeking of liquor. They carried themselves with a cocky swagger, and their mannerisms advertised trouble like a neon casino sign.

Brett Blair, a short, white-trash punk with a Napoleonic complex from a single-parent household in southern Alabama, was the leader and brains of the gang, followed closely by Clancy Gammon, an enormous black youth and the muscle behind the gang. Bam Jones and Todd Barnes, two gangly, illiterate hillbillies, 16 and 17 years old, followed Blair and Gammon like dutiful toadies to round out the group and act as extra bodies for distraction, lookout duty, and general mayhem, while Blair and Gammon schemed plans and made decisions.

Blair was in the middle of a fifteen-year incarceration for burglary, grand theft auto, and rape when he crafted his escape plan and shared it with Gammon on his nineteenth birthday. Blair was an acerbic megalomaniac dedicated solely to the pursuit of hedonism, devoid of any morality, remorse or concern for the welfare of others.

Gammon, a truly gigantic human being convicted of murder for smashing a man's skull with one punch during an argument over a pair of shoes, had sent the nose cartilage deep into the brain cavity. He was two years younger than Blair and stood 6' 7, framed with 385 pounds of solid muscle.

After four months of studying guard rotations and food deliveries in the kitchen, they determined at least two more accomplices would be needed to minimize risk and make the escape a success. Adding more people was a calculated risk, so Blair had two requirements: which inmates he could mentally dominate, and which ones could Gammon easily control physically, smashing them quickly like a couple of bugs, if necessary? Jones and Barnes fit the mold and were approached to join the plan. Two months later, the grand scheme worked and the four older teens escaped through the kitchen in the midst of a routine Wednesday bread delivery during a half-hour window, when the staffing of the guards changed from four to two men.

Blair stabbed guard, Joe Hall, father of two little girls, in the back with a homemade shiv, and Gammon snapped the neck of Bill Morgan who was two weeks away from retirement, looking forward to a Caribbean cruise with his wife. The bread truck was ditched a half hour later for a 2013 Ford Fusion, after Blair slit the throat of the surprised young male driver.

The evening of the escape the boys held up a gas station convenience store, killing the manager and repeatedly taking turns raping the check-out girl for six hours in the back room. Amidst beer and a refrigerator full of microwave pizzas cooked one after another, they savaged the poor young high-school girl in every orifice, over and over again, while Jones staffed the counter, serving customers and pocketing the money for the gang. The convenience store money enabled the boys to sleep off hangovers at a flea bag hotel, where they stole another car around mid-afternoon, and set out on a quest for more money and some food to sponge up their alcohol-saturated livers. Another quick stop-and-rob led them to Nancy's Diner on the outskirts of Andalusia, Alabama.

Blair ogled waitress Shelly in an obviously vulgar manner, as she grabbed four menus to seat them.

"Hey Baby, you are one mighty fine piece of ass. I'd like to chew on yer box 'til yer ears bleed."

Barnes and Jones laughed, and Barnes said, "Yeah, 'til her ears bleed!"

Gammon glued his eyes to Shelly Cox's breasts, clad in the tight pink uniform.

"This way," Shelly said with disgust, rolling her eyes.

Blair elbowed Gammon and laughed, "She's a little spit fire, man! Give me twenty minutes with her and I'll have her speaking in tongues like dat little cunt last night!"

Barnes had an annoying way of always repeating whatever Blair said, "Yeah, that's good…have her speaking in tongues…that's a good one, yeah!"

Blair shook his head, growing tired of the hero worship. At some point, he and Gammon would need to ditch Barnes and Jones.

An elderly gentleman sitting at a table with his wife glared at the gang when they walked by.

"What the fuck are you lookin' at, cocksucker?" Blair said passing, and speaking loud enough for everyone in the general vicinity to hear, turning around to confront the old man.

The man twitched nervously and put his head down, looking intently at his plate.

"That's what I thought. Fuck you, you old bastard! Mind your own bizness!"

Gene Reynolds barely noticed the four hoodlums causing the ruckus. Taking another bite of pie, he slowly sensed the first inklings of relaxation, and the tension in his neck had finally begun to ease. He was slowly able to take full, deep breaths for the first time in over two hours in lieu of the stress filled half breaths that preceded the panic attacks and subsequent over-the-edge occurrences. His pimpled, red-headed waiter, Kevin, a jovial kid with a nice smile somewhat eclipsed by braces, stopped by to refill his ice tea. Gene smiled and nodded, watched the kid walk away, and noticed the four criminals at a table about twenty-five feet away for the first time. Suddenly, he overheard a comment about his waiter.

"…..little carrot-top faggot."

"Yeah, the boys in the joint would have torn up his little asshole!"

"Maybe he'll give us all a BJ before we leave!"

Raucous laughter filled the diner as the boys continued verbally molesting their waitress while ordering their food. Gene's spirits sank and he felt a tiny pang of tension creep back into his neck and shoulder muscles, sensing trouble for the first time, and his meditative journey for peace of mind struggled to continue. With the exception of a young family of five in a corner booth, four other tables of patrons left, or were hastily asking for their checks to leave and avoid a potentially ugly situation. Nancy was vacationing in Florida and her nephew, Bart, was running the diner in her absence. Bart was well-built and did not put up with rude patrons. He would not tolerate the boys' behavior. As soon as one of the servers made mention of it, all hell could break loose, and in this small town, people realized this and wanted no part of it.

A few minutes later, Shelly brought out the boys' food comprised of breakfast for dinner, plates piled high with bacon, eggs, sausage, ham, pancakes, hash browns, toast and jelly.

"Hey Bitch, you ain't got no booze in this joint. Why the fuck not?" Blair bellowed out, as the waitress walked back to the kitchen.

"Yeah, why the fuck not?" Barnes echoed.

"What are you, a fuckin' Parrot?" Gammon said to Barnes. "Every time Blair says something, you repeat it. Ain't ya got no fuckin' mind of yer own?"

Barnes shrugged as Bart walked up to their table. "Hey Guys, you need to tone things down right now because you're bothering other customers, and watch your language!"

The four boys continued their conversation, deliberately ignoring Bart Edwards, who, while not as physically intimidating as Clancy Gammon, had a legendary local reputation for prowess in handling physical situations.

"Are you deaf?" Bart said, raising his voice and deepening his tone.

Blair paused speaking, making exaggerated eye and facial gestures to convey the extreme umbrage taken by the interruption. Turning his neck as if looking at an insect, he said, "You gotta problem, Cowboy?"

Bart was incensed, anger now coursing through him as he bent down inches away from Blair's right cheek bone.

"Look, you cocky, little bastard, you're going to lower your god damn voices and stop disrespecting my servers, or I'm going to thump your ass and throw you out back in the dumpster. You got that, you little shit?"

Blair flinched slightly twice, keeping anger at bay, when Bart said 'cocky little bastard and little shit.' He feigned a forced smirk, fully turning to face Bart.

"You know what Bubba? My eggs were undercooked."

Shelly walked up behind Bart with more coffee. Bart momentarily hesitated shaking his head, stunned by the insolence and audacity of the blond-haired, tanned kid six inches shorter in height, giving up a good fifty pounds to him, should they soil knuckles on each other.

The brief pause was all Blair needed, and things happened very quickly after that. Seizing the short lapse of Bart's focus, Blair lashed out with a vicious back fist to Bart's groin. Bart doubled over and staggered back three steps as Jones jumped up and grabbed Shelly by the throat. Barnes pulled out a pistol, rushing over to the young family of five. Gammon leaped on Bart Edwards, throwing him on the ground and landing four brutal punches to the face, leaving Bart bloodied and unconscious in the middle of the diner close to the kitchen counter area.

Blair leaped up from his seat, throwing the chair behind him on the ground and he, too, whipped out a pistol and shot a round into the ceiling.

"Listen up, mother fuckers!" he yelled. "All of you come over here and lay down on your stomachs next to this worthless turd," he said, pointing the gun down at Bart. "If you don't do exactly as we say, we'll ass fuck you and slit your throats! Barnes, lock the door."

***

The gun shot jostled Gene back to full reality from the temporary cognitive respite. Setting his fork down, he turned to the center of the diner and began to take in the seriousness of the situation. Shouts and screams erupted in the diner, and Gene detected children crying. A very large, muscular black man was jerking his waiter by the hair over to a spot by the kitchen counter where Bart, Shelly, a man, a woman, and three children lie face down on the ground, surrounded by two skinny teenage boys, one holding a pistol, the other a knife.

Gene's heart began to accelerate, as fear began to weave its ugly way through his nervous system like a sputtering electrical current. A voice to his left made him jump.

"Hey you, Buddy? Are you fuckin' deaf or what? Get yer fuckin ass up over there like I said! Move it you faggot!"

Gene looked up at a long blond-haired young man with a scar on his cheek. The young man's handsome looks were soiled by a brazen sneer and look of disdain on his face. As the young hoodlum pointed the gun at him, Gene clumsily fumbled out of the chair, trembling in fear and uttering, "Please don't hurt me. I don't want any trouble."

Blair frowned with impatience and swung the gun against the side of Gene's head, knocking him down, and blood immediately began to flow down his head along the right ear from a puncture gash. Blair kicked Gene in the ribs, yelling, "Get up and get over there, you fuckin' pussy!"

Gene coughed and winced in pain; a small hairline crack in a rib formed from the brutal kicking. He gasped, "Please stop. Please don't hurt me."

Blair leaned down in Gene's face. "Don't disobey or ignore me again or my big black friend will plug your ass with that Alabama Black Snake and you'll be leaking shit the rest of your life. You got that faggot?"

Gene's mind began to drift again. *Why does he keep calling me a faggot? I'm not gay. Do I look gay? I don't think I look gay. Oh God, I can't handle this stress. Why is this happening? Why don't they just take every one's money and leave? Oh God, this is going to make my anxiety come back!*

"Get over there with them!" Blair yelled, kicking Gene in the rear end this time. Gene robotically got up and shuffled toward the prone figures in the center of the floor. Vision was blurring and he was experiencing dizziness. He subconsciously held his right elbow against his side, protecting the injured rib.

As he approached the other captives, Gene's vision slowly began to clear. He saw Barnes, Jones and the enormous black kid guarding the group of five adults and three kids. *My God, they're just a bunch of teenage punks. What are they doing? Don't they know they will go to jail for this?* The brief walk allowed blood to pump in Gene's body, aiding visual clarity, but also escalating his anxiety and stress from the trauma of the situation. He feared a panic attack. Having a panic attack in the midst of these thugs would be a nightmare with an uncertain outcome that could be life-threatening. Gene began to perspire as waves of serious apprehension and alarm set in.

"Lay down, dumb ass," Blair said, shoving Gene in the back, making him land on his knees on the hard tile floor before falling forward on his stomach, exhaling "ugh."

The brazen lead thug took center stage and walked around the prisoners while his henchman kept watchful eyes on their every movement.

"Listen up. I want each of you to get out yer wallets, purses and take off any jewelry you got. RIGHT NOW!" He screamed and smiled as they scrambled in fear, complying with the demands.

Gene took out his wallet and removed the cheap watch and the others followed in kind. Sweat began to drip from his brow and he began to shiver as his trepidation increased.

Gammon could not stop staring at Shelly's figure and the curvature of her buttocks. "Hey, Blair, I'm gonna go over to the corner and tap this white pussy."

"Christ, Gammon! Don't wreck her for me with that monster cock, 'cause I want some too," Blair smiled.

Shelly began to scream and the mother of the family crept closer to her husband on the floor, burrowing into his chest like a badger trying to burrow into a hole. Gammon grabbed Shelly and hauled her over his right shoulder like a burlap sack as she screamed and kicked desperately in vain.

Gene looked up and saw the gigantic boy flip Shelly down on her back by a corner booth diagonally from his line of vision. Gammon tore her clothes off, exposing her ample bare breasts as he roughly forced her legs apart. Fumbling with his jeans, he unleashed an engorged, huge stiffened penis and flung himself into the girl, tearing her open. Shelly screamed in pain and Gene winced, clenching his eyes tightly as if that would block out the atrocity.

Barnes and Jones looked over as the humping black buttocks thrust back and forth like a piston, pummeling the poor girl at a maniacal pace.

"You go Big Boy!" Barnes cheered

"Atta boy Gammon. Tear it up," Jones laughed.

Gene tried to shut out the grunting and screaming to no avail. The lady lying next to the man to his right screamed every time Shelly yelled out in pain, and the children wept in shrugs and gasps. Gene's breathing started to become labored. The rape was reaching a crescendo and Shelly's screams sounded like a tortured animal. Gammon put his hands on her throat, feeling his climax building, unwittingly crushing her windpipe when his seed exploded into her.

The lady by Gene continued to scream in decreasing, slower intervals, but he noticed there was no more noise coming from Shelly's direction. The three men were occupied gathering up their bounty of money and jewelry. A couple of minutes later a sheepish Gammon approached Blair. "Uh, Blair? She ain't movin'."

"What the fuck? What did you do, Gammon?" Blair asked like a scolding mother catching a son tracking dirt across a living room carpet. He rushed over to the girl and felt her pulse. "You fuckin' idiot. What the fuck did you do?"

Gammon just looked down like a little boy caught stealing a cookie, an odd incongruity when coupled with his penchant for ferocious killing.

"Holy shit, he fucked her to death!" Jones laughed.

"Yeah, fucked her to death, "Barnes echoed.

"Shut up, assholes!" Blair snapped. God dammit Gammon, you got to be more careful!" he scolded. "All right, no one gets mommy MILF over there but me," he said pointing to the mother of the family.

The woman began screaming again, burrowing and clinging tighter to her husband.

Patrick James Ryan

"Don't you touch her, you sick fuck!" the husband roared, and the children began to cry again.

Blair smirked down at the man, grabbing and squeezing his crotch, mocking the couple and turned to Gammon. "Hey, lump head, you can make up for it now. Shut his ass up, but don't kill him yet. I want him to have a front row seat to watch, when I fuck his wife."

Gammon took several cloth napkins and tied them together around the man's mouth as he squirmed and twisted in futility to stop the powerful boy. Barnes and Jones were frowning and whispering furiously to each other.

"What the fuck is your problem?" Blair asked.

Jones stammered, "Well, we was wantin' to…..I mean, since Gammon done killed that girl…..I mean, since you said only you could fuck this MILF bitch now…..so what are me an' Barnes gonna do?"

Blair rolled his eyes. "I don't care what you do. You can't have her, so go jack each other off!"

"Well, that really ain't fair," Jones spoke up, stiffening his back in feigned defiance.

Blair smiled. *Well, well. Not such a pussy after all.* "Ok. I get it. Why don't you go bone carrot top boy? He looks like a woman."

"What!" Kevin Dugan yelled in outrage. "Stay away from me. I'll fucking kill you!"

Jones hesitated and looked at Barnes, who shrugged with a 'may as well' nod of the head.

"Well, go ahead, boys," Blair said, waving his hand toward the corner where Shelly lay.

Barnes and Jones swooped in on server, Kevin Dugan, of bright red hair persuasion, and dragged him bucking and fighting to be violated next to the dead girl. Gene watched in horror, now fully realizing his captors' objective was not limited to money, as they seemed dedicated to taking a pound of flesh out of each person in the vilest way imaginable.

Barnes and Jones continued to savage the red-headed server, and the laughter, grunts and noises of wanton, brutal sex made bile rise into Gene's throat. His temples began to throb, sweat drenching his brow and running down his cheeks. Blair and Gammon finished collecting their financial booty and turned to watch the assault on the hapless boy.

"Damn, you crackers ain't got no motion for the ocean," Gammon laughed.

"What the fuck is that supposed to mean?" Blair asked.

"You know, fuckin's kinda like dancin'. Yuh build up a rhythm. Them boys are just bucking like herky jerky whatchama call-its? What's that dizeaze?"

"What the fuck you talking about, Gammon?"

"You know that shit where you jerk round on the floor....? I got it! Epp-a-lupsi!"

You mean epilepsy with seizures?"

"Yeah, dat's it!"

"Pretty funny, Gammon. Hey Barnes, Jones, you stupid assholes fuck like somebody with epilepsy!"

Blair and Gammon laughed as Jones finally finished with Kevin Dugan, who laid bleeding and crying on the floor. Jones and Barnes walked back to the group, sweaty and disheveled.

"You skinny fucks look like he got the best of you!" Blair laughed.

"Nuh uh!" Jones protested. "We fucked his ass real good!"

"Yeah, fucked his ass real good," Barnes repeated.

Patrick James Ryan

"Jesus Christ, Barnes! You are a fuckin' parrot. Stop repeating everything everybody else says! Blair erupted. "Go find a big box or something in the kitchen to stash that pile," he said, pointing to a table covered with the wallets, purses and jewelry.

Gene Reynolds began to gasp and shake, as the first real wave of the panic attack hit. His fellow captives glanced over, afraid he would attract undo attention and accelerate plans for continued sexual abuse.

"What the fuck is that wheezing noise?" Blair asked searching the floor until he saw Gene. "You again? What the fuck is your problem, asshole?" he said in disgust. "I've had about enough of your bullshit, buddy!"

"Wuz up, Blair?" Gammon asked, coming over to stand above Gene.

"This stupid, annoying fuck! First of all, he didn't come over when we ordered everybody to the center. Then he's slow on the draw when I go over to him, pretending to be some retard, deaf mute, or something. Now, he's twitching and gasping like some sick fuck. He's more trouble than he's worth! I've been debatin' whether we oughta just bust a cap in his head right now and be done with him."

"I'll shut his ass up," Gammon said.

Blair stared back in curiosity. "Oh yeah? Whadya got in mind?"

"Well, he's whimperin' like a li'l baby, so I'ze gonna give him a pacifier," Gammon smirked, grabbing his crotch.

Blair cracked up. "Jesus, Gammon, you just busted a nut in that bitch ten minutes ago! Is fuckin' all you think about?"

"What else is there, Hoss? I'ze gonna make him eat me and swallow!" Gammon laughed.

Blair laughed and relaxed somewhat. "All right Big Boy, but I don't want no mess this time......Barnes? Jones? Get the dude up and hold him while Gammon massages his tonsils...and don't kill him, Gammon. I want to fuck him up a little bit before we snuff his ass!"

The dim-witted followers jumped to it with Barnes trailing echo, "Yeah, massage his tonsils. Make him eat him and swallow!"

Gene Reynolds slowly soaked in the lascivious meaning of the words and the obscene, repulsive act about to be perpetrated on his body. His skin began to take on a gray pallor, face clammy with cool sweat still slowly trickling down his brow, snot dripping from his nose, as the gasping for breath continued. An observant bystander with medical knowledge would have surmised Gene was having a heart attack. He continued twitching with involuntary spasms as Jones and Barnes swept in to lift him up. The other captives watched helplessly, bracing for another profane iniquity, while Blair held the gun on them. The three children started to cry again and the mother screamed, burying herself again in her husband's chest, as if it was some type of womb that would shield her from the horror at hand.

"NO, no, no......please don't touch me.....having a bad….." Gene struggled to forms words in whispers in the midst of the high anxiety.

Blair sneered in disgust as his lackeys propped Gene up on his knees. "What the fuck are you tryin' to say, asshole?"

"Got a bad problem......."

"That's right, you pussy little dork. You got some *big* problems!"

"You…..don't…..understand….I…...can't….have ….an…...episode….I …need…...to……"

"Can't have what, dumbass?" Blair yelled, slapping Gene across the face hard. "I don't like you, fuck face! The last guy I met that I really didn't like, I carved him up real good and slit his dick right down the middle. How's that sound, shithead?"

Gene trembled, now pale as a ghost, a nasty red welt forming on his right cheek from Blair's slap.

"Gammon, get it over with. I'm sick of this shithead. I ain't gonna shoot him. I'm gonna carve him up before I fuck mommy MILF over there!" Blair laughed.

Through slit eyes Gene sensed a large shadow looming him, and Barnes and Jones tightened their grips around his arms. The giant young man produced the huge semi-erect organ from his pants again and brought it up to Gene's face, swinging it like a club, striking Gene in the face with a loud smack.

Gene turned his head slightly and heard Gammon say, "Open up now and be a good boy. I'ze got a nice present for ya! Eat this dick, boy! Ize gonna give ya a protein shake to swallow!"

It was at that moment Gene Reynolds officially went over the edge. He turned back to face Gammon, who suddenly hesitated, noticing a diametrically different look on the previously humble, reserved man. Gene's body tensed like he was being electrocuted. Gammon hesitated again, still holding the blood-filled organ in his hand. "What the fuck?"

After that, events blurred as the father of the family of five relayed much later to the paramedics, shortly before he died.

In the course of two seconds, Gene's face contorted in a disturbing way, veins popping out, facial muscles bulging, eyes protruding and turning blood red. His body tensed and froze for a split second, followed by violent muscular spasms and swelling of tissue.

"What the....?" Jones asked in fear, losing the grip on the man's arm.

"Hey, this dude is beefing up like a body builder!" Barnes said, letting go of Gene's other arm.

Gene let out an unsettling growl of pain and discomfort no human would ever make, accompanied by the highly unnatural sound of human bone, cartilage, tendon and various tissues morphing and adjusting to painful reconfigurations. Chest, shoulder, back and leg muscle more than doubled in size, splitting clothing in macabre, musical harmony with the changing tissue infrastructure. Dark brown hair quickly covered his body to complement the horrifying spectacle of a wolf-like snout protruding from his face with long, sharp canine teeth. Hand tissue extended in all directions with fingers lengthening, palms increasing in circumference, knuckles doubling in size, wrists thickening, and nails growing grotesquely long, thick and sharp. Elf-like ears, looking somewhat ridiculous on the now fully formed half wolf - half human abomination, shot upward flanking the murderous red eyes now fixated on the diminishing penis of Clancy Gammon.

The frenzied beast leaped at Gammon, biting the vulnerable organ from the base of the shaft and swallowing it down its gullet as Gammon screamed a cry of absolute terror and pain, while spurts of blood jetted out of the remaining stump of the severed genitals onto the tile floor like a can of spilled paint. The werewolf swung a mighty arm. Deadly, razor-sharp claws opened and extended, decapitating Gammon's head, sending it flying over the kitchen counter into one of the chrome metal coffee makers with a loud clang.

Barnes and Jones screamed in terror trying to run for the exit. The beast was very fast, leaping across the room in strides covering twice the space of the terrified boys. Jones barely had time to turn around before claws ripped open his torso, spilling out intestines and stomach viscera. He stepped back looking down at his dangling innards, having time for a final thought that they looked like a string of Italian sausages, before the wicked teeth tore into his neck, shearing off a huge swath of flesh and rupturing several major arteries. He was dead before he hit the floor.

Barnes tried to back into a corner and the monster pounced on him slashing, biting and tearing flesh, until his face and chest looked like piles of ground beef at the grocery store. No more parroted, fumbling, repeated phrases would emanate from the lump of bloody goo left on the floor.

Screams permeated the diner as Blair and his former hostages scrambled to escape the ferocious beast. Bart Edwards finally stirred halfway out of the stupor from the earlier beating from Gammon, only to look into the face of a movie monster. *Am I dreaming? Some werewolf movie?* The jaws closed in on Bart's neck and the movie abruptly ended.

The young family tried to climb over the counter to hide in the kitchen. The man was lifting his children when the beast caught him, flinging him ten feet into the air against a table, where he broke his back and landed roughly on the floor, head striking the tile. The beast tore open each child quickly, casting them aside for a later snack and swooped in on the mother, decapitating her with another swift arcing blow, holding her upright as it dipped its head into her open neck cavity like a pig at a trough, slurping the blood from the still pumping arteries, and tearing out shards of tasty flesh.

A gunshot rang out, striking the beast in the left shoulder, forcing it to drop the chewed-up body of the woman. The beast howled in pain, and spun around to face a shaking Brett Blair. The cocky veneer was gone, replaced with mind-numbing fear, and the former tough-looking thug appeared five years younger and exposed.

"Get back! Get away, damn you!"

The werewolf snarled, angry, bent on vengeance. Bits and pieces of flesh stuck to its clothing, and bloody hunks of pink tissue and human meat hung between its teeth and matted the hair around its mouth and neck.

Blair pointed the gun again and fired. The bullet hit the beast in the chest, making it stop, hesitate and roar in pain, but it did not go down.

"Jesus Christ!" Blair screamed.

The beast howled for the first time, staring directly into Blair's eyes, and leaped on him, pummeling the thug with a torrent of blows, until Blair's body looked like a farmer's strip of soil that had just been raked and tilled. Then the beast opened its jaws and began to feast on Blair's entire body, tearing off great strips of flesh with the huge claws as easily as someone ripping pieces of paper from top to bottom. Sinking its snout into the prone lifeless body, it began crunching bone, and slurping blood in a maniacal rage. The flesh tasted good, and the beast reveled in the meat and blood amidst whimpers from the man it had thrown across the room.

An hour later, the furious beast finished eating the small children. Their meat was mostly devoid of fat, the sinewy flesh tender and succulent. It took one large bite from the remaining man's leg, but suddenly stopped, growing tired of this hunt. Blood ran down the man's thigh like a shark victim on a beach.

The werewolf stepped over the bodies of its victims, leaving a wake of carnage like a cattle slaughterhouse. It walked over Clancy Gammon last, the perverse irony lost on the beast in its feral state that it had indeed eaten and swallowed Gammon's organ, as laughed about earlier. The beast knew that time was crucial, and it needed to find a safe place to wind down from going over the edge, but it was still hungry. It could not go home as the woman thing had prompted him to go over the edge there earlier in the day, and it had just recently moved its bowels to expel the undesirable parts of her flesh. It suddenly recalled a large open building down the street. The building was called the Mansfield Public Library. Food and prey might be plentiful there.

Stepping outside, the beast cast an ominous shadow against the cement wall of the diner, illuminated by the bright, full moon. Spitting out a small chunk of human gristle intertwined with a torn piece of Blair's shirt caught in its teeth, it arched its back, lifting the blood caked snout, and howled at the moon.

Patrick James Ryan

✝
Spider

"Nice throw Bobby!" Ted Harrison beamed at his young baseball prodigy, when the fastball slammed into the catcher's mitt with a loud smack, making Ted's palm sting and pride swell simultaneously. He slightly struggled out of the catcher's crouch, upon hearing a barely audible click in his right knee from an old high school football injury, and raced across the lawn to hug the thin, sandy-brown-haired eleven-year-old son.

"Absolutely awesome, Bobby! You have one whale of a fastball. Coach is gonna love it when the season starts. Since last summer you have gone from just a thrower to a real pitcher, just like my favorite ballplayer when I was a kid, Nolan Ryan!"

"Nolan Ryan! You really think so, Dad?" the blue-eyed boy grinned like a starry-eyed dreamer. Bobby lived and breathed baseball and knew all the great players, both past and present, and eagerly tore through books about older, legendary ball players like Babe Ruth, Lou Gehrig, Ted Williams, Joe DiMaggio, Hank Aaron, Willie Mays, Sandy Koufax, Bob Gibson, and Mickey Mantle.

"You bet, champ! You really have some natural talent…..but remember my two rules…."

"I know, Dad. Make it fun and work hard to get even better."

Harrison laughed at the hint of pretentious maturity beyond the boy's age. "That's right, Bobby! Nobody ever made it to the Majors by sitting around watching video games all day long. Also nobody usually makes it if it becomes a chore, so work and make it fun! How about if we do one more round and then go see what your mom's fixin' for dinner?"

"Great!"

Bobby ran back to the makeshift pitcher's mound erected by Ted with a couple bags of sand and top soil. A Little League length piece of two-by-four was pounded into the soil at each end in an effort to reproduce as authentic a mound as Bobby would play on in real games. A sudden breeze kicked up, making the cool late March air ruffle their sweatshirts and pant legs, while carrying a distinct odor from the industrial plant down the road from the Harrison's Farm. The odor started in the Fall, a peculiar sulfur smell that Ted and his wife, Julie, noticed on several occasions and now had become a part of their lives. Ted got back down in the crouch, wincing slightly at the pulling of the cartilage again from the right knee. He was going to have to see Doc Emerson about it before corn planting season hit next month.

The Harrison Farm was situated in the small township of Bradenton, Pennsylvania between the cities of Hazelton and Berwick, encompassing most of southern Schuylkill County, totaling about three thousand families. The only other commerce aside from farming was an industrial soap plant about a mile and a half from the Harrison Farm. The Harrisons owned roughly four hundred and fifty acres, planting and harvesting corn, beans, soybeans, and wheat, and tilling fields northwest of the family residence. Approximately a football field to the south was a valley that dipped into a dense three-acre forest.

In addition to the Musashi industrial plant, the only other noteworthy structures in the vicinity were a huge Penitentiary five miles east of the Harrison Farm that contained some of the most hardened, violent criminals in the state locked behind bars, and the local Bradenton School Campus, which housed kids from three counties for grade school, middle school, and high school. Ted was a proud fourth-generation farmer, struggling in the current economy, doing his very best to make ends meet, take care of his family, and groom Bobby to perpetuate the lineage of the farm.

"Okay champ, let's see that ole fastball fire in here," Harrison yelled, smacking his fist into the mitt.

Bobby went through his wind-up motion and threw another perfect fastball that smacked into the mitt with an even louder smack. Ted winced noticeably this time at the power of the pitch, concentrating more on the soreness of his palm, as he threw the ball back to Bobby. "Excellent toss again, Son!"

Unfortunately Ted's aging joints, and in particular, a right shoulder impingement, prevented his accuracy from being anywhere close to his son's ability, and the return throw to Bobby sailed over the boy's head and rolled under the wood pile next to the garage.

"I'm sorry, Son! My bad. Guess I'm getting old!"

"That's ok, Dad. I got it!"

Ted smiled and the eager youngster ran over to the wood pile. *What a terrific kid! We are so blessed,* he thought as the boy sprawled down on the ground on his stomach and reached under the wood pile with his right arm to retrieve the ball.

The abnormally large two-and-a-half-inch female Brown Recluse spider awakened at the shuffling of the wood around her web as the adjacent egg sac containing hundreds of her offspring was noticeably jostled. Sensing danger, it quickly became alarmed and lowered its body, withdrawing the two legs in a defensive posture, keenly alert for any threat to her domicile and safety of her children. Unusually aggressive due to recent chemical exposure, it broke normal protocol deciding to fight the intrusion in lieu of fleeing.

Bobby could not see the baseball and he strained to find it under the wood pile. He panned his arm back and forth hoping to make contact. If he could find the ball and retrieve it without having his dad come over, he knew more praise would be heaped on him. Bobby thrived on his father's praise like an addictive drug. Straining, his fingers grazed the back of the garage and the edge of the baseball. He also grazed what felt like a huge spider web at the same time. Leaning in until his cheek was almost touching the outer piece of a chunk of wood, he was finally able to grasp the ball. He may have subconsciously felt the little legs hop down on his knuckles, and maybe even the teeth sink into the web of flesh between his index and middle fingers, but after sweeping the ground under the wood pile and scraping his young hand over jagged pieces of wood, loose sticks, stones and debris, nothing seemed out of place or unusual about the contact.

"Got it!" he proudly exclaimed, pulling back from the wood pile.

Patrick James Ryan

"Atta boy! I knew you'd get it! Let's toss a few more and go in for dinner."

***

Dinner was excellent. Bobby wolfed down double helpings of Julie Harrison's ham loaf, Stove Top dressing and green bean casserole, while his little sister Karen, age four, fussed and played with her food. Ted Harrison was still flying high about what he hoped would be the second coming of Nolan Ryan. His thin, generous face was still gleaming red with excitement and a sheen of sweat still clung to the brown hair above his brow.

"Honey, you should have seen Bobby hurl that ball. He's got a great fastball and I can't imagine any boy his age having a chance in Hell of hittin' him this year!"

"Ted, the children!" The auburn-haired women with pouty lips scolded her husband for the curse word.

"Sorry, Honey. I got carried away. You should have seen him! You'd of struck out Willie Mays or Mickey Mantle today. Right, Bobby?"

"You bet, Dad! Can we toss a little more tonight after we do the dishes for Mom?"

Ted looked over at his pregnant wife, close to a month away from delivering their third child and shook his head. "We've got to go get some things at the store for your mom after supper and we are going to early church services tomorrow, because Grandma and Grandpa are coming over for lunch."

Bobby's bubble of enthusiasm cracked and he frowned. "Ah, Dad, just for a little bit?" he pleaded.

"No, Bobby. We need to go over to Wal-Mart and get a slanted pillow for your mom, because the baby is really pressing on her belly and Mommy's not sleeping too well."

Bobby looked at his mother, who smiled warmly at him. "Honey, tomorrow after lunch, you can give all of us an exhibition of your pitching power," she said to the disappointed boy. "I know Grandpa would love to see it. Right, Ted?"

"Definitely! You know Grandpa pitched a couple of 'no-hitters' in high school?"

The boy lit up like a Fourth of July sparkler. "He did? Really? I thought all Grandpa did was farm?"

Ted laughed. "It seemed that way to me, too, when I was growing up. Dad was in the fields before I got up and still there when I sat down for dinner, but he was quite a good ballplayer until he hurt his shoulder. You see, they did not have the kind of medicine we have today and after he got hurt, he had to quit playing ball. He also taught me how to shoot a shotgun and revolver. Some day we'll go out and I will teach you how to shoot, too! Yeah, your grandpa was quite a ballplayer. Who knows? Maybe he would have sat beside Ted Williams or Joe Dimaggio if he hadn't hurt that shoulder.

"Wow! Ted Williams and Joe Dimaggio! That sucks Grandpa hurt his shoulder!" the boy said without thinking.

"BOBBY! What did you say?" the horrified mother asked.

"Uh, uh....I meant to say, That's bad. Sorry, Mom!"

"Where did you hear that word?"

Patrick James Ryan

Now, Bobby had heard the word "sucks" about a million times at school and on television, but instead blamed it on his friend, Joe Skinner.

"Well, Molly Skinner is getting a call from me tomorrow afternoon!"

Familiar with his wife's prudish views on profanity, all Ted could do was roll his eyes, finally weighing in. "Honey, don't you think you are overreacting just a little bit? I know you are uncomfortable and your hormones are raging, but his friends are saying that word all the time."

"Ted, why are you defending such vulgar language?"

"I'm not defending it. I just think we don't need to blow it up and call the Skinners. Bobby, we shouldn't talk like that. Now apologize to your mother."

"Sorry, Mom," the boy said sheepishly.

Julie Harrison leaned back in the kitchen chair, rubbing her swollen belly through the blue maternity jumper. "It's ok, sweetheart. I'm just getting testy waiting for your little brother to arrive and get out of my big belly! I feel like Jabba the Hutt!"

"*Star Wars!*" Bobby nearly shouted. "You remembered one of the characters!"

"Yep. Jabba's the big fat one that was trying to get Han and Luke in *Return of the Jedi*. See, Mommy's watching when you think I'm sewing or cooking. I like *Star Wars* too!"

"You're awesome, Mom! Most moms don't know that! Wait 'til I tell Joe and Ryan! Can I be excused to start dishes and then go outside for a while?"

Julie smiled. "Ok, but stay close to the house, because you're going to Wal-Mart pretty quick after dishes with your dad."

***

Fortunately, Wal-Mart was not crowded. Unfortunately, Ted was having a hard time finding the type of pillow Julie could place between her legs and sleep on her side to relieve the pressure from her engorged belly. Finally, a very nice store clerk took them over to the maternity section explaining those types of pillows were not located in the bedding area. Ted thanked her and suddenly noticed that Bobby was not beside him anymore. A woman screamed and Ted scrambled down the aisle toward the sound. Bobby was leaning against a rack of coats with his head down. Sweat poured off his face and hair, and Ted noticed a large pile of vomit on the tile floor below his son.

"Bobby! Are you okay?" he asked, rushing up to his son, as a group of nosy bystanders stared and made a wide berth from the chunks of puke, the sick kid and distraught father.

"Jesus, you're burning up," Ted said, feeling Bobby's beet-red forehead and cheeks. Flecks of vomit coated his shirt, pants and tennis shoes.

"I'm sorry, Dad. My stomach hurts really bad. I don't feel good."

"It's okay, Son. We'll get outta here and get you home. You must have caught a flu bug somewhere."

The nice lady clerk already had a custodian over with a mop to clean up the mess. Ted asked if she could grab one of the pillows and ring him up with his Visa card while he helped Bobby out to their Chevy

Patrick James Ryan

Tahoe. Ted raced the Tahoe home quickly, running stop signs and lights in an effort to get Bobby inside with a trash can before he barfed again in the truck. He was sure Bobby had acquired a nasty flu bug. By the time they pulled into the gravel driveway, Bobby was delirious, mumbling unintelligible words.

He picked his son up and carried him inside. Julie was still in the kitchen, baking a cherry pie for tomorrow's lunch. When she saw Bobby, she dropped an empty cookie sheet on the floor and gasped, "What happened?"

"He puked in Wal-Mart and he's burning up with fever."

"Oh, no! Let me get some Tylenol for the fever."

"Hopefully he can keep it down. Grab some warm 7-Up while you're at it, Honey."

It took about a half hour to get some Tylenol and 7-Up into Bobby's system, and get him into bed. By then, Ted and Julie were exhausted. Ted promised to set the alarm for 2:00 AM to check on him. They placed an old metal trash can next to the bed in case the vomiting returned. They checked on him one more time at 11:00 PM before going to bed and he appeared to be sleeping, but still somewhat feverish.

At 2:00 AM Ted lethargically pulled himself out of bed to check on Bobby as planned. There was a fresh pile of vomit in the trash can and Bobby's hair and pillow were soaked with sweat. He was also sucking his thumb, something he had not done since he was three. As Ted glanced at the thumb sucking, he noticed something odd between Bobby's knuckles next to the thumb in his mouth. Ted leaned in to get a better look. Two small puncture marks surrounded by an angry red area on the skin approximately the diameter of a pencil eraser were clearly visible. The wound looked like a bite from some type of insect; a spider, bee, wasp or yellow jacket. The spot looked like it was also starting to blister. Ted looked down at his son with a worried expression. *What the hell is going on here?*

***

At 4:30 AM Ted got up to milk the cows and check on Bobby again. The bedroom smelled like old vomit and pungent sweat. Bobby was drenched in perspiration like he just hopped out of the pool down at Riley Park. Incoherent, he mumbled unintelligible whispers in between sucking his thumb. The two puncture marks around his knuckles were starting to turn black with angry pus-filled blisters, while the redness and swelling had now travelled up the back of the boy's hand, close to the wrist.

"Jesus Christ!" the worried father exclaimed, running back to the master bedroom. "Julie! Julie! We've got a serious situation with Bobby. Come look at this!"

Julie Harrison slowly came out her dream. During the last trimester she had been experiencing intensely erotic dreams, and in this particular dream she and Ted were making love in a hot tub, and she was riding on top of him, just about to scream out in orgasm before the interruption.

"Julie? Julie? JULIE….! WAKE UP!" Ted gently shook his wife until fully awake and helped her climb out of bed.

Awakened by the commotion, little Karen opened her door and stepped out in the hall in time to hear her normally calm and serene mother scream, and uncharacteristically curse.

"Oh my God! What is that shit on my son's hand? We've got to get him to Doc Emerson." Julie collapsed into her husband's arms staring at the ugly red and black blisters on Bobby's hand, oblivious to Karen crying in the hall.

Ted looked down at his wife and frowned. "We don't have time to wait until Doc Emerson's office opens. We gotta get Bobby over to County Hospital now!

Get Karen dressed. I'll wrap Bobby up in a clean blanket and take him down to the truck."

***

The young intern stood outside the doorway of the triage emergency room with a grim facial expression. He looked like he was only a few years older than Bobby Harrison. The name tag on the lapel of his green scrubs said, Dr. James Graham. He smiled at the distraught couple, as the auburn-haired woman clung to the tall, lean brown- haired husband. The man held a sleeping, mini replica of his wife, their daughter, Karen, in his arms.

"Mr. and Mrs. Harrison, it appears Bobby has some type of insect bite. My initial guess pending lab results would be a Brown Recluse spider, based on the appearance of the bite and his symptoms. We've had a few Recluse cases over the years, but I honestly can't recall a reaction of this magnitude. The venom really moved quickly and Bobby's a very sick boy at present."

"Is my boy going to die?" Julie Harrison whimpered, tears streaming down her rosy cheeks.

"No. I think you got him here in time. I've cleaned and scrubbed the wound, scraped away some of the dead tissue around the knuckle and back of his hand, and ordered a strong round of antibiotics and a low dose of steroids to keep the inflammation at bay."

"I thought spider bites typically only affected babies and old people," Ted said.

"That's usually a good rule of thumb to go by, Mr. Harrison, but nature is very unpredictable. Bobby's asleep right now and I would suggest you go home and get some rest. By mid-morning, the first round of antibiotics should be kicking in, and I am optimistic that we will start to see a change for the better in his condition."

***

At 8:30 AM, the phone rang at the Harrison Farm. Dr. Graham advised the Harrisons to get to the Bradenton General Hospital immediately. Bobby's condition had taken a turn for the worse and a specialist from Philadelphia was flying in. Julie quickly called her sister to watch Karen at the house, and they rushed back to the hospital. By 1:45 they were still waiting in the reception area of the Children's Ward when a tall, thin, distinguished man with a salt and pepper beard, wearing John Lennon style glasses approached them with Dr. Graham. The man was holding a folder with Bobby's name on it.

"Mr. and Mrs. Harrison, this is William Campbell, Chief of Infectious Diseases at Children's Hospital of

Philadelphia and a renowned expert on the treatment of insect and animal bites."

The tall man bowed and shook hands with the worried parents. "Let's go over to the Conference Room over here," he said pointing to his left.

While they were approaching the Conference Room, a nurse rounded a corner with a hospital gurney carrying Bobby. The young boy's normal cherub face was masked by a deathly pallor, and puffy like skin more reminiscent of a pumpkin than a boy.

"Oh my God," Ted Harrison gasped.

"Bobby!" Julie screamed.

Dr. Graham stepped between the hysterical woman and the gurney in the hallway while onlookers in the Waiting Room gawked at the commotion.

"Bobby is on his way to intensive care on the eighth floor. He's having some additional reactions, but we feel with Dr. Campbell's assistance that we can stop the spread of the infection and kill the venom."

"Why can't I see him?" Julie wailed.

"You can shortly, but he is heavily sedated and would not be able to speak right now," Dr. Campbell said with calm, commanding effect. "Please, Mrs. Harrison. Let's go in the Conference Room and discuss what is going on."

Reluctantly, the Harrisons watched their son being wheeled down the hall and followed the doctors into the Conference Room and Dr. Graham shut the door.

"Mr. and Mrs. Harrison, I brought Dr. Campbell in because he's dealt with some of the most serious of bites ranging from insects, poisonous snakes, frogs, and rabid animals. He is a renowned expert. About an hour after you left, Bobby's entire body began to swell up with fluid. We call that edema in elderly people who have poor circulation, but for a young healthy boy like Bobby, the only possible cause would be an infectious agent in his blood stream. That is when I called in Dr. Campbell to take over Bobby's case. I'll turn it over to Dr. Campbell now, as he has already made a clinical evaluation and examined several blood tests we've performed on Bobby."

The elder physician smiled and took off his glasses, making him look immediately a little younger and at the same time, slightly less intelligent.

"First of all, I am very sorry for the grief you are feeling, but I am confident we can heal Bobby and get him well again. Spider bites can sometimes be a tricky thing. After examining the wound and the blood work, there is no doubt Bobby was bitten by a Brown Recluse. It is unusual for a Recluse to be this far north. Most cases are easily treated. What is still concerning me about Bobby is that his blood work and labs indicate he absorbed almost twenty times the normal potency of venom we typically see in these bites.

"Good God! Twenty times? How is that possible?" Ted asked.

"What does that mean?" Julie asked her facial features narrowing with growing fear.

"Well, this particular spider must have been a real nasty specimen. Have you seen any spiders around the Farm?" Dr. Graham asked

"Sure. I mean we leave in the country and have a farm. There are spiders everywhere."

"Of course. I'm sorry. Let me clarify. Have you noticed any unusually aggressive spiders? Spiders getting into the house? Any of the cows with bite marks or signs of infection?"

"No. Not at all. We usually see Daddy Long Legs, but they run from us."

"Did Bobby play outside the day his symptoms appeared or the day before?" Dr. Campbell asked.

"Yes. He and I were tossing the baseball yesterday afternoon. He's got a hell of a fastball for his age!"

"I am sure he does," the elder doctor smiled. "By chance did he roll around at all on the ground or venture into some tall grass or a wood pile?"

"Yes. One of my return throws when we were playing catch yesterday afternoon sailed over his head and he had to dig into the wood pile to retrieve the ball."

The doctors looked at each other.

Ted leaned forward. "Why? Is that important?"

"Do you think we can capture the spider if it is, in fact, in the wood pile?"

"I don't know. I can look. I'm not totally sure it happened in the wood pile. Why?"

"Well, there are many things we can learn like…." Dr. Campbell began.

"Having the exact spider can help us run some tests to see exactly its size, type, specific strength of its venom, and other items that would benefit us in Bobby's treatments," Dr. Graham stated quickly.

Ted noticed a quick glance from Dr. Campbell, as Dr. Graham put his head down, to look at some charts. The brief, unspoken professional rebuke told Graham his youthful exuberance was writing checks his limited bank account of experience could not cover. He reddened down to the middle of his neck, fumbling with the chart and Campbell continued. "Sometimes the effects from bites can be nothing at all; other times they can be immediate as in Bobby's case, or even delayed for days. Many people are not even aware of the bite. Let me walk you through what can happen so you will understand what we are dealing with for Bobby, and why Dr. Graham called me in.

When a reaction occurs from a Recluse bite, a small white blister usually appears. In some severe cases, within the next twenty-four to thirty-six hours, a reaction may occur that is characterized by restlessness, agitation, fever, chills, nausea, weakness and joint pain, all of which happened to Bobby. The first thing to understand is that the damage done by a Recluse spider bite is done by enzymes in their venom that liquefy human issue. Antibiotics are usually not effective unless bacteria are discovered. However, in Bobby's case we have discovered both his chemical enzymes at a very high level, and several types of bacterial infection are present. I think this is why he is having such a severe reaction. Bobby was bit close to the knuckle and we suspect both venom and bacteria have invaded the bone, causing an infection in the bone."

Campbell paused and sighed, allowing the Harrisons to digest the case history before dropping the big bomb. "The other item unique in Bobby's case is that the venom does not appear to be destroying tissue, but for some reason it is entering and mutating the tissue."

"What?" Ted asked.

"What does that mean?" Julie asked, her mouth hung open in an "O" shape.

"What I mean is that it appears the venom is blending in with Bobby's cells. The cultures we have taken have shown cells that have both spider and Bobby in them."

"Oh my God!" Ted cried out as Julie started to weep.

"Now, now, it's not the end of the world," the older man soothed. "My plan is to take the knuckle bone out and replace it with a portion of his hip bone. This will get the infected bone out and kill any remaining infection. He is young enough to have it mend and still be a great pitcher in the future. Then we will blast the area with anti-venom that is being flown in. He looks so swollen right now, because his body is naturally producing tons of white blood cells to fight the infection, He's also on a pretty high dose of steroids to keep his strength up."

"Will the anti-venom work?" Ted asked, leaning forward in the chair.

"I believe it will. I've not had a case where it has failed."

"So, you think you can cure him of all this?" Julie pleaded.

"Yes, I do. I've worked a dozen cases where anti-venom treatment has worked. It may take a couple of weeks in the hospital, but I think we will get it in time. This is a very unusual reaction. Bobby has around seventeen infectious bacterial agents in his system right now, and many of them don't typically accompany bites from insects or animals. That is why I wanted to see if we could capture the spider."

The Harrisons went home and tried to resume normal activities. Ted went through the entire wood pile and could not locate any spiders. In fact, the entire pile was devoid of anything with the exception of a couple of bloated dead squirrels that stunk so bad, Ted almost vomited when he disposed of them.

During the following week, Bobby's condition began to improve slowly. The anti-venom that was administered seemed to be killing the venom released from the bite. Dr. Campbell successfully performed the bone surgery to remove Bobby's knuckle and graft the small piece of hip bone piece in its place. Bobby was awake, coherent and even eating solid food again, including buckets of ice-cream to his pleasure, constantly asking when he could go home. The Harrisons were immensely grateful and relieved.

***

After thirteen days in the hospital, Bobby came home to a party of relatives, neighbors and friends. While still weak, he was able to play with cousins and class-mates. He ate well, assimilating back to near normal activities as much as could be expected. Around 10:30 that same evening, and long after guests had left, he put away his baseball cards, drank a ninth glass of water, and went to bed, eagerly looking forward to a day of swapping cards with his buddies tomorrow. As he fell asleep, his last conscious thought was to get up and have his tenth glass of water.

***

The tiny collection of venomous cells that migrated to Bobby Harrison's right shoulder's deltoid tendon barely clung to life. Most of their brethren had been brutally destroyed by a combination of hostile invaders that inhibited their ability to follow their genetic marching orders. In their limited capacity to comprehend rudimentary survival, the cells felt the threat of imminent extinction. But wait. A very recognizable friend was now awash in the organism. Water from the Harrison well, mixed with the infiltration of dihydrogen monoxide, also known as DHMO, from the industrial plant flooded the organism's tissues, muscles and tendons. Like lighter fluid to fire, the tainted water flowed through the cell membranes of the near dormant venom, awakening and revitalizing the cells like the father welcoming back the prodigal son. In one hour, cell mitosis was cresting. In three hours, venomous cells equaled 1/5 of Bobby's normal cells. By the wee hours of the morning, venom permeated throughout Bobby's entire body, destroying all the anti-venom in his system and initiating the process of total cell mutation. Around 3:30 AM Bobby woke and began to prowl around the house.

***

Julie Harrison woke with a peace of mind she had not felt in days around 7:45 AM. She remembered her mother's words of wisdom, when she was at a crossroads in life during college. "Julie, adversity is a great teacher, and prevailing over it can be one of life's greatest accomplishments."

Julie smiled with a deep sentiment of love and looked over at the empty bed, smiling again this time in admiration of her husband's tireless work ethic. Ted was a truly noble man, selfless and dedicated. She marveled at how he could get out of bed so early and milk the cows after such a long day of excitement, and a mixture of concern about Bobby's safe return home. Bobby had clung to her most of the evening when they returned from the hospital, reminding her of how he would burrow into the blanket and snuggle with her, while she and Ted watched TV when he was a toddler.

Julie was sure the trauma of the experience prompted some insecurity, and she relished the chance to mother him again. As she rolled off the bed, she felt a sharp itch on her right shoulder from what must have been a bug bite or a mosquito bite. *Damn mosquitoes*, she thought, reaching to scratch an enlarged white blister on the back of the shoulder. When she straightened up, her mid-section was hit by a significant contraction. She immediately recognized the stomach pain. *Oh no! I can't be going labor this soon!* When she straightened up, another contraction shot through her torso, making her double over in pain, sidling over to the window nearest the barn.

"Ted….? Ted….? TED….! Where *are you?*"

There was no answer. The barn door was uncharacteristically closed and none of the normal cow milking sounds could be heard. Another violent contraction tore through her womb, dropping Julie to her knees. A warm trickle of liquid dribbled down her left leg. The blood was bright red.

Oh God, I'm losing the baby! "TED! TED! WHERE ARE YOU!! TED….TED!

***

Ted Harrison was following the tracks that led into the woods approximately two hundred yards from the southwest corner of the farm for forty-two minutes, when he heard the ambulance.

Earlier, Ted woke with the alarm at 4:00 AM to milk the cows at the regular time. Light rain softly pelted the siding on their bedroom window. Julie was sound asleep, looking peaceful and content. He had smiled, gently kissed her forehead, and headed down the hall to look in on Bobby. He was not in bed. He wasn't in the bathroom either, or anywhere else in the house after a quick review. He ran back up the steps and discovered that Karen was not in her little bed with the pink Cinderella comforter either. His heart began to pound, sensing something was seriously amiss.

Looking in on Julie quickly, he decided to let her sleep and not alarm her. She was five weeks to term with the baby and the whole spider bite ordeal had upset her greatly. *Where in the hell are the kids?*

He checked the barn, the vehicles, behind the house, the corn field, and basement twice. No luck. He dashed back in the house and grabbed a flashlight. It was while walking back to the vehicles that he noticed the two sets of muddy footprints leading down the driveway. He quickly began to follow the prints. Approaching the woods, his mind ran amuck. *Where are they? What in the hell are they doing out in the rain so early in the morning? Bobby had explicit instructions to stay in bed and rest today! Karen is never up this early. What the hell is going on here?*

Ted picked up the pace and began to trot. Brambles, thistle and weeds smacked the legs of his jeans, as he followed the twisting path. Abruptly the footprints stopped where a patted-down stretch of foliage branched off to the right.

Ted took three steps into the foliage, when he finally heard the ambulance siren.

***

Ted had never met Doctor William Golding, Chief of Staff for Obstetrics brought in for difficult deliveries and premature births. Julie had been in labor for over fourteen hours, and things were not going well. Golding's bedside manner was lacking, but he more than made up for it in getting the job done. Goldman's entrance into the room gave Ted a tiny sense of relief for the first time since witnessing the paramedics lift Julie off the floor amidst a puddle of blood on the bedroom carpet. Goldman brushed aside the resident OB, "Young man, if you want any hope of saving this child and the mother, get the hell out my way and assist when I ask."

Glancing over at Ted, he frowned. "Sonny, we got some problems here, but we will do our best to stabilize your wife, get the baby out now, and hope for the best. You can stay over in the corner and don't ask any questions or interrupt, no matter what happens. Right now, every second is precious."

"Yes sir," Ted said obediently.

"Nurse, she's losing too much blood to fast," Dr. Golding grimly stated. "I need to set up a transfusion and prepare for an immediate Cesarean, if we have any chance of saving this baby and keeping her alive. Get Doctor Baldwin in here to administer a general anesthetic pronto."

"I think Doctor Baldwin is already administering in OR Four."

Patrick James Ryan

The normally serene and calm elderly obstetrician glared at the young nurse and snapped back, "I don't give a shit if he's shooting anesthesia up the Pope's ass. Get him in here RIGHT NOW!"

"Yes, doctor. Right away."

Ted Harrison watched the nurse scurry out of the room and looked at the pale face of his wife with agony and concern. It had only been twenty minutes since the ambulance arrived at the hospital, but it seemed like another day as Julie had been shuffled from three different rooms before entering this operating room. Ted called his brother to look for Bobby and Karen and bring them to the hospital, once they came home from fooling around or were found, which ever came first.

The nurse came back with an agitated anesthesiologist who stared at Dr. Golding. "Jesus, Bill, I got yanked out of a tough case. What the hell is going on?"

"Scott, I've got no time for diplomacy or bullshit. We can talk later, and if you're pissed, tough shit. Shut up and do exactly as I say, or we are going to lose both mother and child here. I need you to set up a general ASAP, as time is of the essence. We can't wait on an epidural!"

Ted watched while Dr. Scott Baldwin applied his expertise with the anesthetic, and three OR Nurses prepped Julie with a second IV bag of O Negative blood, as the pain medication dripped into her system. Julie was still conscious and very afraid, whimpering, but would soon be sedated for the birth of her child. The surgical drapes were slid to block her view of the surgery should she awaken, and a catheter was inserted into her bladder. Ted stood in the corner in blue surgical attire feeling helpless.

Dr. Golding applied the most common procedure known in obstetrics as the low transverse incision, or bikini incision to the general public. Golding preferred it because of the lower incidence of blood loss and infections. Ted watched Golding make an incision across Julie's belly approximately two inches above the top of the bikini line.

"Ok, the first incision is going well. Blood pressure is stable. Fetal ultrasound looks fuzzy, probably because of all the uterine blood clotting around. Let's open up the uterus and get this baby out."

Golding delicately cut through the tissue of Julie's uterus, exposing the interior of her womb and the baby. He paused, his eyes narrowed, and a troubled look could be detected under his mask, as his brow creased. Suddenly his eyes opened wide and he stopped the procedure.

"Oh my God!" one of the nurses screamed.

"What the fuck is that!" Dr. Golding grimaced, backing away one step.

"Jesus Christ, it's eating the tissue in her womb!" Baldwin shouted.

Ted felt adrenaline shoot through his trunk and his heart was close to popping out of his chest. "What is it? What's wrong?"

"Stay back! Stay back!" Golding yelled.

Suddenly a fountain of blood from inside Julie sprayed up in the air just missing the overhead lights, as something severed her bloated uterine artery, filled with blood from the late-term pregnancy.

Patrick James Ryan

"Get me some kind of bag or net!" Golding shouted. "Jesus Christ, what the hell is that goddamn thing!?"

Ted broke the stated protocol and rushed the operating table just in time to see the head of a grotesquely deformed, hairy child with eight yellow eyes and long black fangs hanging from a deformed mouth. Flanking the hideous mouth were two hairy-appearing legs propped up over the edge of Julie's bloody stomach starting to pull itself out of her body.

Ted gagged and forced bile back down his throat, tears streaming down his face. The closest nurse bent down and threw up on the floor by the right side of the bed. The infant mutation perceived this moment as a threat and a web shot out from one of the legs, wrapping around her neck. The thing leapt to her throat, sinking its fangs deep into the soft flesh. She screamed and fell to the floor, twitching as venom a thousand times more potent than a normal Recluse paralyzed her, death setting in seconds later.

Ted and Doctor Baldwin ran to the cabinets across the room, searching for anything that would serve as a weapon while Dr. Golding tried to reach the exit. The other nurses also began to scramble for the heavy OR doors, only to be quickly wrapped in web silk from the mutated spinneret glands in the beast's legs, rendering them trapped and motionless. Golding slid under a gurney to avoid the deadly silk.

The medium-sized dog-infant-spider-thing pitter-pattered across the tiled floor toward Ted and the doctors.

Dr. Baldwin held up a bed pan and threw it at the thing, striking it across its bloated, hairy white abdomen, displaying the telltale Recluse fiddle black line down its back. The bed pan hurt the thing and it backed up, a hissing sound emanating from its mouth, followed by a putrid smell of dead blood from deep inside its body. A greenish, foul-smelling pile of urine and feces spilled out of the rectum of the thing, a mostly human organ, but lacking the ability to separate the two waste products in its current state.

"Christ, that's fuckin gross!" Baldwin cried.

Taking advantage of the creature's bodily function distraction, Golding ran to one of the medicine cabinets, ripping the door open and grabbing two large, stainless-steel instrument trays.

He tossed one over to Baldwin who immediately placed it over his face, carefully walking toward the monster. Golding approached from the other side, as Ted stared in complete disbelief at the entire spectacle, glancing from the monstrosity that was to be his child to his butchered wife lying on the bloody operating table.

Baldwin approached the thing, ready to slam the instrument tray down on top of its head, while shielding his eyes, face and neck. Suddenly the silk web flew out, wrapping around Baldwin's legs, locking them together and dropping him to the ground. Before Golding and Ted could respond, the thing sprang through the air and sank its fangs into the left side of Baldwin's face. The pitiful anesthesiologist twitched and writhed on the tile floor for several seconds, as blood drained from his face and then death quickly set in.

Golding and Ted stared in disbelief for another three seconds and then Golding rushed the thing, swinging the tray like a madman...screaming. The monster sprayed out another web, catching the tray and yanking it away from the older doctor like a parent swiping a toy from a child. Two more bursts of silk web engulfed Golding's torso and neck. The beast sprang again, sinking fangs into the top of Golding's head while he screamed with horrifying pitch.

Ted Harrison finally broke out of the stupor with an anger that was all encompassing. Like a man possessed, he grabbed one of the IV poles by the upper end, ripping off the bag and tubes and advanced on the spider-thing, slamming the heavy steel down over its body as it attempted to feast on Golding's skull, brain and heart. A crushing blow thundered down on its back as Ted heard and felt the distinct squishy sound of penetration. The monster howled and Ted yanked the pole out, dragging flesh and green, spewing blood over his head for another strike. The wounded beast backed off Golding's lifeless body and slunk toward a corner to hide. Ted was now faster than the wounded abomination and pinned the beast's body against the wall with the four legs of the IV stand's bottom frame. Hissing, the beast raised a leg to spray a web. Ted pressed in with all his might as the four legs from the stand compressed into the monster, further pinning it against the wall and forcing its leg down. It began to wiggle around madly trying to free itself. With a maniacal shout, Ted lunged in again, pressing his whole weight behind the thrust.

The creature's eyes bulged for several seconds until abruptly it's head and abdomen exploded like a burst water balloon, spraying green blood and viscera all over Ted, the floor, the wall and Golding's dead body. Ted ran back to Julie and felt her wrist. Her stomach was splayed open like the twisted peak of a volcano. Blood, pink and yellow tissue, and folds of loose skin lay in a haphazard display of gore. Ted closed his eyes, fighting tears and released the wrist. The body was already getting cold.

"I am so sorry, my love. I think I know what is going on now and I have to leave you, Honey, to take care of it."

He bent down and kissed her forehead, pausing to look back one more time at the mangled torso of his wife. The battered and forlorn husband dashed out of the room, heading for the hospital exit hell bent on putting an end to his nightmare.

***

Shortly after 10:00 PM, Ted drove the family Truck 70 miles per hour, tearing through stop signs, and traffic lights. He swerved to avoid pedestrians at a manic pace to complete the twenty-minute drive back to the farm to find his children, mentally clinging to the remote hope that his worst fears had not become reality.

The hospital was in total chaos, people running up and down the halls screaming; security guards running to the bloody operating room; medical personnel pushing gurneys and portable credenzas stacked with supplies. Police sirens pierced the air as cruisers descended on the scene of the carnage, closely followed by the town news team van. It was easy for Ted to run out the nearest exit and sprint to the truck without being noticed.

Gripping the steering wheel, he looked down at the streaks of red and green blood on his arms and bits and pieces of the preternatural slaughter assaulted

Patrick James Ryan

his mind. *What the hell happened? It's not possible! How could this happen?* As Ted drove, reality began to set in and the adrenaline rush from the traumatic events in the hospital operation room wore off. Tears streamed down his face, as Ted raced the truck across the highway back to the farm.

"Why God...? Oh God, Julie! My beautiful wife! She's gone. A fuckin monster killed her and took my baby boy! My life's destroyed! Why God! Why...!? How could you let this happen?"

Fifteen minutes into the drive, Ted's tortuous anguish began to turn. Like a tiny flicker of flame that eventually evolves into a forest fire, anger swelled deep within him, a burning rage against evil forces that were destroying his family filled his soul.

It's that goddamned fuckin' plant and all that chemical shit they're spreading everywhere! It's messing with nature! God damn them!

Slamming down on the accelerator, the car shot up to 80 miles per hour as he finished the drive. Peeling into the driveway, he saw his brother-in-law Joe's jeep in the driveway. The front flood lights had been turned on, illuminating most of the house and lawn, casting a hue at the end of the lawn and out to the barn. Ted leapt out of the truck, not bothering to shut the door, and ran into the house. He nearly jumped down the basement steps and then grabbed the key to the gun cabinet. Taking the 12-gauge shotgun out, he opened a backpack and loaded it with a generous supply of slugs. Moving quickly to his desk, Ted grabbed a .45 long Colt hand gun, loaded it with rounds, and added a heavy box of rounds into the backpack. Finally, he scooped up his buck skinning knife used for deer hunting. Running back up the steps, he grabbed three towels from the kitchen, the flashlight, lighter fluid, and a poker from the living room fireplace. Finally, he ran upstairs and put on a long sleeve shirt, sweatshirt, and scarf around his neck. After a final check, Ted flew out the front door, guns and backpack in tow, pausing momentarily to scan the area before starting down the driveway toward the path into the woods. His brother-in-law Joe was nowhere in sight. He failed to see the sinister shadow slink along the side of the barn and slither into the bushes.

***

Flying through the woods along the path to the patted-down foliage, Ted had the uncanny sense twice that he was being watched. It was the same intuition people sometimes get in the wilderness, when a bear or a mountain lion is stalking prey. On both occasions he stopped and listened, panning the flashlight in all directions to the front, rear and both sides. There was no movement or sound, not even insects. Under the circumstances the sound of his breathing sounded like a locomotive in the eerie silence. Pressing forward, he finally came to the same spot where the footprints ended and lead off to the right where the grass, weeds and accompanying foliage was no longer matted down, and dense foliage and darkness loomed deeper into the woods. Sighing, Ted proceeded with caution into the uncertain wilderness.

***

Patrick James Ryan

The thing had quietly been stalking Ted Harrison since being interrupted in the barn, when the truck screeched into the driveway. Supremely intelligent and gaining knowledge every hour, its combined insect and human genetics gave it an extraordinary gift for cunning and stealth. The man was following an earlier path made when the thing had not yet fully transformed into the magnificent creature and supreme hunter it had evolved into during the course of the day. Without question, the creature knew the man posed a threat and must be stopped. Deftly moving parallel to the man through the foliage like water through a stream, it could easily take him out any time it wanted to, but that would be too easy. It had bigger plans for the man. Twice the man stopped and scanned the area. The thing sensed detection and froze, but the man's limited senses were not capable of discovering it. The man would prove to be a good test for future encounters and the mutated thing smiled. The man was old and out of shape, no match whatsoever for the thing as it watched him stop, panting for oxygen and rubbing one of his extremities with a pained look on his milky-white face. Soon the man would pick up the pace again and walk into the nice surprise waiting for him!

***

Ted struggled to navigate through the dense wooded area. The foliage made it difficult to see farther than ten feet ahead with the limitations of the flashlight. The evening moon was largely eclipsed by cloud cover, making the journey more difficult in the unnerving, eerie silence. The arthritis in his right knee was flaring up, making the navigation through the uncertain terrain of woods more challenging. The hefty combination of the backpack housing the equipment and gun, and the shot gun strapped across his back began to feel like a ton of bricks and he was forced to stop again. Sucking in the fresh air, he gave the old, worn cartilage in the knee a rest. The flashlight in his hand resting on the left hip uncovered the silhouette of what appeared to be a stone structure that looked like a small cave about sixty feet diagonally from his current position. There was matted foliage leading toward the cave.

"What the fuck? How can there be a cave in the woods?"

Cautiously, he approached the stone, taking off the backpack and setting up the contents, sensing an unfathomable, unimaginable encounter, unique in human experience. Flashes of the bloody scene from the hospital cut through his mind, and he readied the shotgun and handgun, placing the knife in its sheath through a belt loop. Ted wrapped the towels he put in the backpack around the fireplace poker, generously squirting the lighter fluid on it with determination. Whatever lay in wait for him was going to get a battle.

In his heart, he knew Bobby was gone and Ted was determined to put the abomination of nature down and send it back to the hell it came from. Emotionally, devoid, his only hope was to rescue Karen. Sighing one last time, he made sure the safety switches were clicked off on the weapons and began the walk into the cave.

Peering inside the mouth of the structure, he realized two things. He would need to duck to walk inside, and the cave was even darker than the woods.

Patrick James Ryan

Taking the Bic lighter from a pocket, he lit the end of the poker to illuminate the cave, and crouched down low enough to enter. The cave twisted around several times through tight passageways, and the vastness of the tiny structure was deceiving from the outside.

Finally, he came to a larger opening and held up the flaming poker, panning it along the floor, ceiling and walls. Something moved about ten feet in front of him against a wall. He flashed the flame again and gasped, nearly losing balance and falling down. Karen Harrison was strapped against the wall cocooned and unable to move with several layers of the same white silk the baby monster had used at the hospital. She appeared to be dead when Ted approached. As the flame got closer, her eyes suddenly opened and took several seconds to focus. With relief, Ted rushed forward.

"Karen! Karen! Are you okay sweetie…? Daddy's here now. I'm going to get you out of here."

"Daddy? Help me." The traumatized little girl whispered.

"Yes, Honey. I'm here. Let me get you out of here."

Ted Harrison's daughter slowly came out of her daze and looked directly into the eyes of her loving father with a level of maturity uncharacteristic for her age. "Oh Daddy, you need to get out of here. It's too late. Bobby's done something to me. He'll do it to you too. You need to get out of here now!"

Something behind Ted moved in the periphery of the cave. Ted turned and caught a glimpse of something very large crawling across the opening of the passageway. Turning from Karen, he flashed the flame and the monster was revealed. Bile rose in Ted's throat and he puked up the deli sandwich he'd eaten earlier at the hospital cafeteria. Gasping for air, he heard a voice that sounded like a person trying to speak with sand in their mouth and throat; a gravelly, deep, rough voice that made a chronic smoker's hack sound like a soprano.

"Hi Dad! Are you Okay? I was hoping we could toss the ball around a bit," the thing mocked.

Ted soaked in the features of the abomination with a mixture of fear and loathing. Bobby's handsome youthful face had mutated into a hairy mess. Five black eyes rested above a grotesquely deformed nose flanked by three more eyes above a mouth with two extended fangs that hung halfway to the ground. Eight hairy legs replaced the human legs he was born with, attached to a swollen stomach. Its back was now a brownish white. Purple slime dripped from its fangs, forming a solid puddle at the base of the thing's head. Repulsed, Ted brought up the shotgun from behind his back.

"I wouldn't do that just yet, Daddy-O," the thing mocked again. "I've got a big surprise for you in just another minute or two. Don't we, Karen?"

Ted was stunned at the maturity and condescension in the monster's voice and demeanor. "You mother fucker! What did you do to her?"

The spider-boy actually looked like it was smiling in its own repugnant way. "Take a look, Dad. All those kids you and Mom wanted are about to, how should I put it - pop out!"

Ted heard a rustling to the rear where Karen was attached to the cave wall. Whirling around he saw her body begin to convulse and shake. Sweat poured off her body profusely and her face was flushed, beet red like a deep sun-burn. Suddenly the skin around her neck began to split open. A small slit evolved into a larger slit and blood oozed out in a slow trickle gathering momentum until it was spouting out.

"Oh my God!" Ted screamed. "What the fuck did you do to her, you sick fuck!" He spun around and noticed the thing had already closed half the gap between them.

"Don't fight it, Dad. Join me. It's so cool. I can do so many neat things now!" the monster said in its gravelly voice. "Ah, my brothers and sisters are arriving."

Ted turned back to Karen and noticed tiny baby replicas of the monster begin to pour out of the torn tissue of his daughter's neck. Karen was clearly dead and her body was spawning hundreds of the little monsters that would quickly grow into dog-sized freaks of nature, terrorizing the countryside.

"Jesus Christ! What in the hell!?" Ted screamed. Tears and screams burst from the heavily distraught father as several more tiny spider-like things sprung from Karen's neck.

Ted's shock quickly turned to anger. "No!" he whispered.

Then he shouted, "NO!NO!NO!NO!NO!" *This must stop now*, he thought. Bringing up the poker, he reached toward his daughter.

"I'm sorry, Honey!"

Before the flame could reach her, a painful grip grabbed his right wrist. Ted looked down to see the silk web wrapped around it. He dropped the poker and more deformed miniature spiders popped out and began to crawl toward him. A shadow loomed above him as the Bobby thing approached, fangs dripping the slimy coating.

"NO! NO WAY!" he screamed, struggling to reach the poker with his left hand before the flame went out. The mutated hybrid that was once his beloved son was tugging at him with the silk around his wrist toward the fangs.

Using tremendous effort and strength he did not know he possessed, Ted reared up and kicked the creature in the face. He strained to reach the poker, swinging it in an arc across the floor, where the swarming little replica spiders crawled. As the flame hit them, Ted heard small sizzle sounds, almost like popcorn cooking and popping in a pan. Enraged, the monster tugged again, but Ted swung the flame across the web silk, cutting it in half. A portion still clung to his wrist and dangle below like an extra appendage.

Thrusting the flame forward again, Ted gained a second when it backed off to completely torch Karen's body and the remaining spiders. The creature howled in rage with a piercing, unnatural sound like metal grinding against metal in a car accident. Web silk shot toward Ted from four different directions as he rolled on the ground to avoid it, dropping the shot gun in the process.

The fire was spreading across the cave wall as Karen's body burnt along with the layers of spider web that made up her cocoon. The flames cast a macabre light for the cataclysmic battle between father and monster son. A web strand wrapped around Ted's leg. Another shot toward his neck, barely missing. Straining, he was able to grasp the Colt .45 revolver in time right before the monster sprang on his leg attempting to sink its fangs into his flesh.

Patrick James Ryan

The incredible strength of the monster on his leg made any shot difficult, and the first bullet blew off one of the legs, while the second bullet sailed over the thing's head. Hissing, it stumbled in to close the kill, tugging violently on Ted's leg, jolting him so hard he hit his head on the ground as another shot rang out when he was roughly jolted toward the beast, dropping the pistol.

Dazed from slamming his head, Ted looked up to see the last stray bullet had blown a huge hole in the creature's face, a lucky shot taking out three of the eight eyes. Green blood spewed from the jagged, cratered hole, and the monster collapsed, breathing heavily. Ted looked around for the gun and saw it was out of reach several feet behind him. Reaching for the knife in his belt loop, he saw the monster slowly try to raise itself up. Too weak to speak, its eyes communicated surprise and shock, as the mouth and fangs strained to reach any part of its Father. Ted unsheathed the knife and sawed through the silk around his leg, leaping back before a deadly bite could penetrate one of his legs. Scurrying back on his hands and legs like a crab, he found the .45 and stood up, walking cautiously toward the creature. It looked up at him with a pathetic, resigned look in the undamaged, bulging eyes in its torn body.

"You are not my son, you sick, disgusting fuck!" Ted cried, pumping the remaining rounds into the monster until it was dead. Panting, he tore a portion of his shirt and grabbed the still flaming poker and torched his biologically mutated son. Flames crackled and a noxious smell permeated the cave, forcing Ted to gag and head down the passageway back to the path and the farm.

It took him nearly twice as long to get back home as it did to get to the cave. He lost the flashlight during the fight, his right knee was throbbing with every step, his head throbbed painfully, and he was dizzy from the concussive blow on the floor of the cave. Nasty bruises and abrasions were forming on the exposed skin of his left leg and both wrists had bloody ridges where the web had wrapped so tightly on his flesh. At one of the stops, he decided to reload the Colt in the event he ran into anything else. Finally, he saw the flood lights from the house in the distance and felt a deep sense of relief that he was almost home. He planned to hop in the truck and drive to his sister's house in the next county and get away from the farm.

As he approached the property, he heard the cows in the barn screaming, mooing and kicking their stalls. Ted ran toward the barn, tore open the door, turned on the light, and rushed inside, abruptly halting in his tracks. The entire barn was cluttered with dozens more of the dog-sized spider mutants like what had become of his son. Ted's brother-in-law Joe hung on the barn wall above the tractor in a cocoon, his neck torn open with a huge bloody gash. Several of the spider-things were attacking the cows, sinking monstrous fangs into their soft flesh. Four turned toward Ted as he screamed out loud at yet another scene of carnage that was quickly becoming too much to bear. Ted blew the head off of the first spider that approached and burst the abdomen of the second, readying himself for a third shot before attempting to make a run for the truck. A hissing sound to the rear made him spin around. Four more of the dog-sized half-spider half-human beasts blocked the exit from the barn. Only two more rounds left. No way out. He shot the middle spider in the entrance way, blowing its head off to see if the others would move. No such luck as the other two began to advance toward him. Ted looked around the barn and saw the monsters pop up from every corner of the building. Raising the gun with painful resignation, he put the gun in his mouth and sent the last bullet through his brain.

***

Lucretia Jordan looked at her co-anchor, Phil Hershbarger, and smiled. "Well, WHRX News in Philly was first on the scene for an interesting story today about spiders."

"That's right, Lucretia," Phil chimed in. "Apparently, there has been a pretty bad outbreak of Brown Recluse Spiders in rural parts of eastern Pennsylvania. We have team coverage reporting on this interesting event. First up is Reporter Dennis Wilcox who has just arrived in the city of Berwick. Dennis?"

"Good evening, Phil and Lucretia. We have heard several stories of very large Brown Recluse spiders behaving in unusually aggressive ways in this part of the state. As you may know, the Brown Recluse Spider has a nasty bite that can even be fatal for the very young and the very old. Healthy people are also encouraged to seek medical treatment, if they suspect they have been bit by a Recluse. Local authorities have stated that they plan to spray affected areas to minimize the spread of the spider population. There were a couple of reports of some deaths in the township of Bradenton about forty miles from here.

Officials are denying any fatalities and not commenting further at this time. Back to you, Lucretia"

"Thanks, Dennis. Our team coverage continues with Molly Carlson who interviewed Dr. Unger Vanderbark, an entomologist at Temple University. Molly?"

"Lucretia, we visited with Dr. Vanderbark, one the most notable experts on insects in the country this morning in his office."

"Doctor, how likely is it for a Brown Recluse to openly be aggressive with humans and other animals?"

A distinguished, gray haired gentleman with old-fashioned horn-rimmed glasses, frowned. "The Recluse gets a bad rap because it is known to have a nasty bite. But just like the honey bee who will not sting unless provoked, the same applies to spiders, including the Recluse. When threatened, it usually flees to avoid a conflict, and if detained, may further avoid contact with quick, horizontal rotating movements to escape before biting as a last recourse. I have been studying these insects for over thirty years, and every now and then, someone has an unusually bad reaction to an isolated bite and panic ensues. I am sure these news reports are more hype than fact."

"Well, Phil and Lucretia, there you have it from an expert. This is Molly Carlson, WHRX news."

"Well, Lucretia, now we have some clarity. To hear some of the stories we heard today, you'd think Brown Recluse spiders were dashing across the state spreading havoc."

"That would be awful! I hate spiders!"

"Don't worry, if we see one in the news room, we can just swat it with our papers!"

They both laughed as Phil continued. "In other news the Dow was up today, and the S & P 500……"

Puzzles

I am uncharacteristically vexed at present over the complexities of the various puzzle pieces arrayed before the humble concrete floor in my basement, so I am taking some respite to share some long pent-up thoughts in my trusty journal that I keep for posterity and on the slim chance that someone close to my intellect will discover it, should something happen to me.

Let me begin by sharing the background of my deeply sacred passion in an effort to shed insight into my unique psyche and distinct mental capacity. I apologize in advance to any reading this account, who in their asthenic minds may view my prose as peremptory or unduly pretentious.

***

At a purely baseline level, I must start by stating that I love puzzles. I always have. The stimulus to the brain, the quest to solve a problem, the joy of the journey, the worthwhile consumption of time that eclipses reality associated with puzzles have always mesmerized me. As I look back and reflect on the personal journey to the success I have now, I am left to surmise that Dr. Childress was the first person to legitimately recognize my unparalleled intellectual prowess. I often wondered if Dostoevsky latched onto something tangible in his descriptive, literary rhetoric of Raskolnikov being an extraordinary man since I certainly identified as such throughout my entire life, whether a singular observation or collective depending on who was involved in my life at the time.

I experienced what social liberals would colloquially call in sterile-slang language a rough upbringing. My birth parents may have suspected in their limited capacity my affinity to high intelligence as I was growing up, but most likely did not understand the eccentricities and wrote the skills off as mere oddities. In their defense they had shortcomings too profound and insidious to comprehend anything beyond a vulgar, ubiquitous existence. Blue-collar upbringings, a pervasive lack of reading and culture, and overall complacency with mediocrity nicely sums up their extreme mundanity. These imperfections precluded them from any significant involvement in nurturing abilities beyond toileting, feeding, and of course, copious amounts of corporal punishment, embedded in their bellicose approach to life. Frankly, they were not endowed with any remote capacity to fathom the capabilities of a person with an IQ of 204.

Now please forgive my condescension and do not misinterpret my criticism of them to be anything other than candid descriptions from objective clinical evaluation, as I harbor no ill will toward them. The meek and feeble-minded have their niche, too, and I would never deny the common man his due! After all, they were my parents and I desired their love, anticipating every day the family would aspire to my hopes and dreams.

I must confess, though, that it did cause some frustrations at the early age of six, when I was already reading Dostoevsky, Camus, Chaucer and Ayn Rand for leisure, while pouring through the works of Plato, Aristotle, Mill, and Nietzsche for intellectual stimulus. When compared to their *TV Guide, Soap Opera Digest* and local newspapers penned by writers who could only be viewed by anyone with even a basic education as apostates of an elementary vocabulary, I felt very lonely. At odds with my love for them was the growing attitude of pity for the inadequacies and repugnancy of their personas, which were fraught with mental underachievement.

Their Neanderthal existence consisted predominantly of vacuous interludes of television viewing, excessive alcohol consumption, and debate over such sporadic, nonsensical matters like sporting contests with the occasional segue into apoplectic fisticuffs of violence, as they tore into each other over such banal issues as to which one would control the television remote control, or who would eat the last piece of pizza. I must admit their temerity, ignorance, and indifference toward notions of self-actualization, metaphysics, utilitarianism and existentialism drove me at times to choleric episodes, where I smashed the demeaning toys they bought for me and carved slivers of wood out of the bed frame with kitchen knives and used the pieces as puzzles to put back together. My favorite solace was putting together a thousand-piece puzzle on a flat card table in my bedroom when my stupid father was able to buy one at a garage sale. Puzzles helped me problem-solve and stay sane. My puzzles gave me a sense of order in that hillbilly environment.

In what I now refer to as a mercy killing, my father was murdered in a convenience-store hold up, buying the last in a ceaseless case of beer that he

Patrick James Ryan

drowned his life in like a dry sponge in a wet sink every night, when I was eight. My mother was ill-equipped financially and emotionally to care for me and my sister, Shelly, an annoying cherub faced lump of goo cast in the epitome of my parents' worst traits. In spite of being a worthless sloth, I tried to love Shelly too. I often postulated, but never asked, if I was adopted. I still ponder adoption even to this day.

At the risk of being a cliché', home life reached critical mass about seven months later with an ensuing emotional boiling point when Shelly died under mysterious medical circumstances with a rare drug found in her system, culminating into the last straw for Shaw County Children's Services on the heel of numerous complaints from neighbors against my Mother for neglect, abuse and malnutrition.

So at the age of nine I was removed from the home and placed in a plethora of foster homes, some nice, and some not so nice. I remember one older, grey-haired man and his wife, who took me to church every Sunday, piously smiling at everyone during the services, and then taking turns raping me every night during the week.

"You think you're so smart, but you don't know anything, Boy!" The man would grunt, as he reamed my insides out, while the woman laughed and clapped like a high school cheerleader, taking Polaroid shots for future masturbatory escapades.

Strip away their perverted, unabated, carnal lust and coarse hypocrisy, and the substance of their existence was an opaque, empty shell. Luckily, they had several large puzzles of *The Last Supper* and *The Crucifixion* to keep me occupied, when I was locked in the bedroom and not being abused.

As I moved on to other "caregivers," one young, fat woman made me eat laxative- laced chocolate chip cookies, until I either threw up or had relentless diarrhea. I remember her constantly screaming, saying the same trite phrase: "You ungrateful, dirty, messy little boy! Look at this mess. I took my valuable time to make you my delicious cookies and this is the thanks I get? You just shit your pants and have no control! Drop your messy pants and underwear now, Mister!" The paddle came out after that for a good two minutes non-stop, or until I either bled through the scarred, pus-filled bumps on my bottom cheeks, whichever came first. Whoever wrote *Beowulf* must have had this woman in mind when conjuring *Grendel*. I used to steal her dishes and smash them on the basement floor, forming my own puzzles to put them back together to mentally escape the abuse.

Eventually, neighbors would finally notice oddities and parenting that was not conforming to social norms, which would precipitate intervention from Children's Services into the next household and foster home.

At the age of twelve, one nice couple, seemingly unable to have children of their own, treated me like a crown prince. I was able to read, speak openly, attend a good school and continue to advance my intellect. I was so happy! I thought I had finally found a home and the loving family I longed for all my life, until one day I heard them excitedly discuss the woman was expecting a baby.

A year later I was placed with a cold, middle-aged couple who viewed me as a paycheck to buy more alcohol and cigarettes, otherwise ignoring me. In six months the most challenging periodical available for

Patrick James Ryan

me to read was *National Geographic*. Ultimately I became a ward of the State during my teen years, and was at least able to achieve a free education at a private state prep school on the tit of the tax payer, a small price to pay for the abuse I bore over the course of all the years after separation from my mother.

The government doesn't do much well, but I must confess that I received a better than an average education on their dime. Taking advantage of accelerated course offerings, I learned French, Latin, German, Spanish, Japanese, Chinese and Russian fluently, and easily comprehended advanced physics and mathematics by the tenth grade. Math, in particular, intrigued me. At the risk of being too condescending and crudely braggadocious, I must confess that the most famous mathematicians and physicists like Poincare, Archimedes, Galileo, Kepler, Descartes, Newton, and Einstein bored me. I was able to grasp each of these so-called esteemed men's theories as readily as a slot player can read a neon Vegas sign!

Throughout these years of enlightenment my puzzles were a constant companion. After I received a Doctor of Philosophy in Mathematics at M.I.T. in 1995, I was recruited to work for the CIA solving some of the most sophisticated codes and data encryption systems the enemies of the United States have ever devised. I quickly acquired a reputation as a master puzzle-solver. I cracked many of the major codes in several of America's notable conflicts from 1995 to 2003. In my spare time my passion for puzzles grew into obsession, solving puzzles of all types for solace and stress relief. I easily swept through and mastered a variety of board puzzles, word puzzles, logic puzzles, and even the famous Raymond Smullyan's presumably difficult logic-inspired puzzle in a mere twenty minutes. I grew quickly bored with Sudoku. Mazes, games and riddles at best were frivolous time-fillers. I had an obsessive thirst, almost a physical ache, for something that would both challenge my intellectual curiosity and stimulate my interest. Please do not take my words and explanations as arrogance, as I was quite surprised myself how simple the supposedly complex came to me. I merely longed for puzzles that had both emotional significance tied to my upbringing, and some semblance of difficulty.

On one dark day I made the naïve mistake of casually mentioning over lunch my cerebral gallantry and some of my other personal beliefs to some superiors in the government. Unfortunately, I became an immediate object of skepticism, derision and scorn. Ultimately, treatment by my associates culminated into perturbation with extreme alienation like a pariah or a leper. I was forced to be "examined" by a buffoon of a psychiatrist way below my mental capacity, who interviewed me for six days and figuratively stabbed me in the back, advising the National Security Advisor it would no longer be in the nation's best interest to keep me on staff. No appeal. No negotiation. No opportunity to inquire. I was gone. Period. Imagine that? I was left to the whim of an unqualified middle-aged, ferret-faced psychiatrist with dimples as large as potholes and verbal skills akin to a pregnant moose giving an opinion on my worthiness to contribute to high level government projects. It was tantamount to a person with chronic catatonia weighing in on the artistry and creativity of

Patrick James Ryan

Da Vinci. I was completely flabbergasted at their dismissal.

I spent the next ten years like a Bedouin. I migrated from institution to institution and incompetent shrink to incompetent shrink like a frequent air-traveler until I finally landed at the New York State Institute of Deviant Behavior, a politically incorrect and highly challenged, draconian facility that was perpetually under the watchful eye of the liberal elite. The facility was attacked not only for the institutional name, but the harsh methods employed to "treat" patients. Its massive dark, ivy-stained brick walls and morose décor housed some of the most nefarious minds in America. It was during my stay at this lovely Hanoi Hilton for the hopelessly insane that I met Dr. Enrique Childress.

Dr. Childress seemed to genuinely want to listen to my story from our very first meeting. He was both interested and empathetic. We had in-depth conversations on philosophy, science, the arts, mathematics, religion, and of course - the efficacy of puzzles. In fact, Dr. Childress placed special focus on my passion for puzzles. During our time together, he theorized that my obsession with puzzles was a way to escape the pain of childhood and repress the emotional trauma of addressing reality versus the deep hidden desire to have a loving family. While an utterly simplistic and clichéd theory, it was a straightforward rationalization and had plausibility, although I am still not sure I buy his premise. How would I have been blessed and satiated with so much intellectual prowess, if concerns over family trivialities drove my success? I eventually concluded the good doctor's theory, while well-intentioned, was sheer nonsense.

Dr. Childress went to great lengths on my behalf to acquire some of the most complex and difficult puzzles in the world. The puzzles helped me remain content for about a year, and I even won an international contest during incarceration against several European puzzle champions for completing a large, 3-D, double-sided white, opaque 5000-piece puzzle in six hours. Eventually, I grew bored with Doctor Childress's commercial puzzles and began to explore alternatives. One day I had a sudden revelation of how to sequester my own puzzles with the aid and assistance of some of my sanitarium colleagues. I worked on these puzzles in the basement laundry room floor, and it caused quite a stir among the inmate population. Word of my awesome puzzles became the talk of the facility. I decided to keep these puzzles hidden from Dr. Childress, because he had been so kind in getting me so many commercial puzzles and threw a big party with cake, when I won the contest. The poor man thought in earnest that his puzzles were a challenge for me, and I did not have the heart to tell him they were boring in lieu of my self-created puzzles.

Unfortunately, one day Dr. Childress found my puzzles and took offense at them. Our discussion about them turned into argumentation, and I realized Dr. Childress was holding me back, trying to control me with his puzzles. The realization was both enlightening, as it exposed his limited intellectual capacity and causative for me because it proved to be a catalyst for action. I knew it was time for me to leave. Now you might be thinking that it would be hard for someone to leave a highly secured asylum, but not for a person with extraordinary intellectual dimensions.

I made my plans, organized myself, and chose the face of a pesky, gorilla-like custodian who would be just perfect for the package I needed to take with me. A quick dose of chloroform, facial mask fitting, and I was wheeling out a seemingly mute patient with facial cuts in a straitjacket, posing myself as an orderly. Not one person glanced at me twice and I strolled right out the front door on the grounds to join all the other orderlies wheeling loonies around in the hot August sun. When the mail truck arrived at noon, I grabbed the wheelchair, and hopped into the back of the truck. The mailman was still on the seventh floor delivering the monthly psychiatry periodicals to all the doctor's offices, when I told the double Y chromosome guard at the gate to have a nice day, flipping him a copy of somebody's girlie magazine for kicks.

The departure from the asylum was three months ago. I now reside in a deserted farmhouse in northern New York State, earning a humble living at a grocery store, working on mastering my own challenging puzzles. These puzzles are the most complex and sophisticated I have ever laid mind to, and I am filled with renewed passion and zeal for life as a result. So now you understand my background and have perspective on just how special my intellectual contributions could have been to the world.

***

The pieces before me have better clarity now. The opportunity to put thought on paper, however archaic and confining writing may be, has apparently sharpened my focus. I think I am ready to proceed with the puzzle. In fact, I am getting a very good mental vibe and I may just get my hammer out to create some more pieces to solve.

I am almost done with the right rib cage of Dr. Childress. The custodian's face that I cut off from his skull fit nicely over Dr. Childress's unconscious face, when I escaped from the asylum. Amazingly, the security there is so lax that I was able to wheel him out like any other patient and load him into the mail truck without any interference.

Anyway, now I've got a challenging puzzle. The bone fragments slivered and splintered poorly on the bumpy concrete basement slab, unlike the smooth textured tile in the laundry room basement at the asylum where my puzzle pieces broke into nice, ornate uniform units. I really should not lament the past, as the newer fragments from this basement are certainly much more challenging. If my clarity lasts, I may be able to piece together Dr. Childress's spine and skull by the end of the week. With some luck I'll have his puzzle finished completely at month's end, and I can place him next to the completed puzzle of my sister, Shelly. She fared very well in the rented storage unit over the years, even after I dug her out at the cemetery. Yes, things are going nicely. I think eventually Karen, the checkout girl at the grocery store, will make a fine addition to my happy little family! Her unique facial bone structure might even rival some of the most difficult doubled-sided jigsaw puzzles I've ever solved!

Patrick James Ryan

†

The Lonely Deaths of Booker and Chance

July 30, 1945
(A few minutes after midnight
Somewhere in the Philippine Ocean)

The ocean was calm and serene, looking like glass in the stillness of moonlight. Tyler Booker stepped outside on deck near the stern of the ship for a quick smoke with Walter Chance, as the big cruiser knifed through the glimmering waters of the Pacific at a steady seventeen knots.

"We're making good time for such a hush-hush operation," Booker said approaching his friend.

"Yeah, pretty smooth," Chance said. "She's a decent craft....hey, I'm glad you stepped out 'cause something's been buggin' me I wanted to ask you about."

Booker looked on curiously while Chance continued. "Why no escort, Ty? These waters gotta be crawlin' with Jap subs."

Booker, the thinner of the two men with black hair and strong facial features showcased by a large nose, sighed at what he viewed as another episode of excessive worry by his friend. "C'mon, Walt. You worry too goddamned much! When we hopped onboard in Guam, the Quartermaster said the *Indianapolis* had been on a secret mission and was headin' back to Okinawa. We're movin' pretty damned fast and whatdya think the word 'secret' means?"

Walter Chance, a short, blond-haired man with a thick neck, pudgy face, and noticeable acne scars, in direct contrast to his thinner, dark-haired colleague, frowned and shook his head. "Yeah, I get all that and I guess you're right, but I can't shake a nagging feelin' that we should have waited the extra day and taken the original ship we were scheduled for and passed on this one. We're not even listed as being on this ship, Ty."

Booker was about to respond when a massive explosion rocked the entire ship. KABOOM! Fire rose up over the starboard bow of the cruiser with chunks of metal debris flying through the air. An errant chunk of shrapnel grazed Chance's forehead slicing a cut, and a thin trail of blood immediately began to drip down into his eyes. Booker was thrown against the metal rail, cracking a couple of ribs. Seconds later another explosion blasted the cruiser, causing irreparable damage, and knocking the two men and hundreds of others off their feet. Metal screeched and the ship lurched to the head of the bow.

"OH MY GOD!" Chance screamed.

"Jesus! They're gonna kill us all!" Booker screamed.

Men were running all along the deck, some on fire, others bleeding and torn from the blasts and all the flying metal shrapnel. Screams and shouting filled the air accompanied by ongoing explosions, as fire found its way to electrical outlets and generators. Chance ran into a man with blackened, peeling skin, shards of his shirt melted into the second and third layers. The man was howling a scream that made Booker's spine vibrate as he watched the man fling himself overboard into the water below. Dozens of other men crawled to the stern with various stages of burns, blackened skin peeling and oozing blood and yellow liquid; others lay dead on the deck. In minutes the ship began to list, filling with water at the bow.

A lieutenant ran by, yelling at Booker and Chance, "She's gonna sink. Get down to the marine compartment and get a life jacket...NOW!"

"C'mon, Walt. Let's get the fuck outta here!"

Walter Chance stood up and raced after his friend down the debris-filled deck, filled with shock and horror at the disastrous turn of events.

***

August 1, 1945

The mid-afternoon sun beat down over the ocean like a flame in a candle, making the cluster of approximately 950 men feel like they were roasting in a slow cooker. The water-soaked, sun-drained sailors were scattered around a two-mile radius amidst slicks of oil, debris from their ship, and a diverse consortium of sea life, some harmless, some extremely dangerous.

It had been two days since the Japanese submarine struck gold, when two out of six torpedoes blasted away the bow and starboard side of the cruiser, sinking her in less than fifteen minutes, and throwing surviving men into the Philippine ocean out in the middle of nowhere. Their experience would become legendary; a horrifying tale of disaster, terror, lost life, testimony to resiliency, and survival. In just a day and a half, they lost close to 300 men from drowning, hypothermia at night, searing heat during the day, and a never-ending onslaught of sharks, nibbling, attacking and eating the helpless survivors, floating like sitting ducks in life jackets.

About three miles west of the main group, two lonely men not formally listed as part of the crew, migrated adrift, surrounded by a thick oil slick, giving the heavy, darkened lubricant forms an aerial appearance similar to the eye of a hurricane. The formerly calm stillness of the ocean the previous day had been replaced with a steady wind, creating five-to-seven-foot-high waves, making conversation between the two men difficult, and prompting them to shout, further taxing salt-drenched throats.

"My throat is burnin' from all the damned salt in the water!"

"Breathe through your nose, Walt, and try not to swallow the water. It will fuck you up." Tyler Booker advised his friend through cracked, bleeding lips.

"I tried breathin' that way. I'm all plugged up! Damn sinuses!"

Booker shrugged. "Then I don't know what to tell you. My ribs are fuckin' killin' me. I think I cracked a couple of them."

Walt strained to look across the horizon, as another wave lifted him up and down in a steady rhythm. "How long do ya think it's been since we lost 'em?"

Booker crinkled his nose, already red, cracked and peeling from the hot rays of the sun pounding down the last 54 hours. "I dunno. That huge oil slick separated us from the main group around dawn and we've been drifting this way ever since."

"If we drift too far from the main group, no one will come to rescue *us!*"

Booker bobbed up with a wave. "Quit worrying, Walt! As long as we're stuck by this oil slick, they can't miss us. Remember they need to spot us by air first, and it will take a while to get a PBY out here to get us anyway."

"What about the sharks, Ty?" Chance asked with growing fear and concern.

"We've only seen a couple of 'em and they've been little fellas. Stick to the basics. Focus on right now. Remember what they taught us in basic training, if we end up in the water with sharks? Kick 'em, push 'em away, hit 'em in the nose….and never swim away, cause they view that type of movement as a scared fish. Right?"

"Yeah, I remember. I'm just plain scared, Ty."

"Me, too."

Another seven-foot wave lifted Chance up suddenly and his eyes bulged in surprise. "Jesus! What if we never make it out of here and get back home?" he said.

"Quit thinkin' like that, Walt! I'm sure the Captain sent out a S.O.S. before we sank. The cavalry will be comin' for us soon."

Chance grimaced as yet another wave lifted them up, making his stomach feel like it was plunging to his feet. Recovering, he asked Booker the same question for the fifth time, since they'd been cast adrift. "What the hell do you think happened?"

Booker paused, frowning as the rough sea jostled the sore ribs, riding a wave six feet above Chance, until he came back down. "Jesus, Walt! You've asked me that twenty times! Like I said about an hour ago, I don't know. It had to be some torpedoes from a Jap sub......what else could it have been?"

Chance shrugged and continued to look in every direction nervously. "I dunno. It was such a big fuckin' explosion. I thought maybe a Kamikaze hit us?"

"At night Walt? C'mon, use your head. That salt water messin' with your mind?"

"I dunno what the fuck's wrong with me. I'm so hungry and tired."

"Me too. Fuck, I'd give up my left nut for a glass of water right now! I'm so fuckin' thirsty!" Booker said, succumbing to the pessimistic rant.

"Yeah, my throat feels like fuckin' sandpaper and I miss my girl," Chance said.

"What's her name again?"

"Mary Jo. She's got sandy-red hair and pretty, big blue eyes. I wish I was back on the farm in Nebraska with her instead of in the deep shit we're in now!"

"Me, too. My wife's name's Darlene. We'd only been married a month before the Japs hit Pearl. I used to get some letters, but with all the movin' around I done, they stopped. She probably thinks I'm dead."

"We should have stayed in Guam after loading that cargo. We should never have taken that offer from that Quartermaster to sneak on board. Early liberty in Okinawa ain't worth this! We're not gonna make it, Ty!"

"For cryin' out loud Walt, will you quit the goddamned whining? It ain't helpin' the situation!"

Chance sighed, nervously shifting his eyes across the horizon.

***

The massive fish cruised the water sixty feet below the throng of struggling prey at the surface. The Great White shark shook its caudal fin, thrusting itself faster through the water, honing in on jittery movement at the surface. Its varied, smaller brethren mostly comprised of White Tips, Blues, Hammerheads and an occasional Tiger, gave the monster shark a wide berth out of fear and respect, recognizing immediately the ferocious size and killing capacity of the hungry killing machine.

It had consumed three of this familiar species the last day and a half, jogging its limited memory back to a week spent thousands of miles away many mating cycles ago. Back then it had just been an overly large young, twelve-foot pup off the coast of the American Jersey Shore in the summer of 1916, hunting at the time with its much smaller sister.

The food supply in the area at that time had been abundant, slow and easy to kill, so the sibling Great Whites uncharacteristically hung around the area for more than a week. Without the capacity for conscious thought, the Jersey Shore experience instinctively taught the large male to hunt alone, and it evolved into a rogue hunter from that moment on, recognizing the greater efficiency and ferocity it enjoyed over its sibling and others of its kind. It feasted on three satisfying kills off the Jersey coast, before migrating to the coast of Chile in South America for the next several years. Its sister was not so fortunate, suffering capture and death at the hands of the vengeful species off the Jersey Shore not long after her big brother moved on, so common in the animal kingdom.

The gigantic shark had already lived nearly double the normal lifespan of its kind, learning all the nuances and lessons required to thrive as a supreme predator, feasting on any edible food source crossing its path, regardless of size, off coasts in South America, South Africa, Japan, Oceania, the Pacific Coast of North America, and through the straits of Gibraltar to the Mediterranean sea.

For the past couple of years, it had been attracted to the unique motion of huge, inedible, fast moving creatures traveling the Pacific that regularly dumped food and trash, sometimes making thunderous noise above the surface of the water, suggesting food sources may be present. Bouncing from California to the Hawaiian Islands and Japan, it followed these large, moving creatures, devouring any life it came across. In recent days, one of these enormous creatures dumped a generous amount of prey into the ocean, along with a potpourri of debris and a slimy, slick substance the large predator had not encountered before.

Just shy of 28 feet in length and hovering between 7500 and 8000 pounds, depending on the abundance or scarcity of food sources, it was fully grown and significantly larger than most of its kind. Its killing prowess had been honed to a fine skill unrivaled in the ocean, with the rare exception of large Orcas. It was a consummate hunter and powerful eating machine apart from any shark currently alive. Unlike members of its own indigenous Great White species, it harbored no caution when hunting, using both ambushes from below and straight-on frontal, attacks without fear or a hint of potential danger from prey. The mottled gray upper half of the shark sported several deep scars from encounters with boats and tussles with females of its kind from mating over the years.

Shaking its tail, it accelerated upward to three of the creatures who had drifted from the main pack. In five seconds it was upon an unsuspecting, weakened sailor. The huge mouth opened, unveiling window sized jaws with seven rows of three hundred teeth, adorned with serrated edges.

The sailor, a nineteen-year-old red-haired, freckled farm boy from Circleville, Ohio, was trying to readjust a life jacket, fumbling with the strap, causing haphazard splashes in the water. Twelve feet away, a fellow sailor was instructing him to simply pull the life jacket around from back to front, when the young man was thrust up out of the water, as the huge jaws came crashing down, splitting the red head in half at the waist. A fountain of blood and chunks of tissue flew into the air, on the water, and into the screaming faces of his fellow sailors.

The gigantic fish swallowed the torso and legs of the young man down its gullet without conscious thought, spinning around for the upper half to complete the meal. A four-foot-high dorsal fin broke the surface, followed by a huge conical snout and the upper jaw and teeth of the beast cruising through the water until it found the head and upper body of the young man. The massive jaws opened, engulfing the entire remaining half of the man, crushing flesh, bone, hair and tissue, and dragging the body in its mouth underneath the surface, while the onlookers screamed a desperate, mortified howl of terror.

***

By dusk on the evening of August 1st, Tyler Booker and Walter Chance were exhausted from the tortuous sun, lack of food and water, and pervasive battering of the waves. The silent but never-ending effect of salt water on their skin was slowly eroding the top layer, replacing it with angry, red, painful blisters from exfoliation. The continuous swallowing of little bits of salt water was causing dangerously elevated sodium levels in their blood, and the ensuing delirium was beginning to set in from the excessive salt in their systems, despite their best efforts to avoid it all. Chunks of oil slick, opening up to the sea, broke away from the large, circular spill that had encapsulated them, since the tide carried them away from the main group of survivors.

Two hours after sunset, the stark contrast from searing heat to frigid cold set in on Booker and

Chance one more time. Shivering they rolled around in the vast ocean, wondering what monstrous beast below the waves would come to claim their flesh. Booker grew up in Minneapolis where ice, sleet, snow and sub-zero temperatures made winters long and brutal, but the biting cold he felt penetrating his bones now made Minneapolis seem tame.

Around 3:00 AM Chance started shouting, waking up Booker who was dozing.

"It's a boat…! It's a boat….! Right over there, Ty! See it….? We're rescued!"

He began to swim in the direction of the moon glow over the water. It took Booker a minute to get his bearings and he scanned the area. There was no boat. *Jesus, he's losing his mind. Christ!* He knew Chance was hallucinating from the salt-water ingestion and must go grab him quick before he swam off, bounced into a big piece of debris and got hurt or worse yet, ran into a shark. Fighting the relentless pain in the ribs, Booker swam to Chance, grabbing the confused man. Chance spun around, his face lit with excitement, spittle running down his chin.

"See it, Ty? See it? The boat?"

Booker grabbed Chance's life jacket. "Walt….! Walt…! There's nothing there."

Chance seemed not to hear or comprehend. "I think it's a PT boat. They've come for us, Ty! They've come for us."

"Walt…! Walt!" Booker said to no avail. Raising his right hand, he slapped his friend across the left cheek. "WALT!"

Chance finally paused, taking in his whereabouts and looking at Booker as if for the first time.

"Walt, you said you saw a boat and took off swimming this way. There is no boat Walt....there is no boat."

Chance's face fell and a lone tear trickled down to his nose. "Oh God Ty, I'm losing it....I'm going nuts!"

Booker hugged his friend. "You're not going nuts. It's the salt water we're swallowing."

"Oh God, Ty, I'm so scared."

"I know."

They held each other trying to stay warm, two small and insignificant figures stuck in the vast, never-ending darkness of the Deep.

***

August 2, 1945

The Great White circled the little cluster of six men, huddled together as the morning sun pounded down on the surface. It had consumed two dead men during the night that had passed away from hypothermia and been relieved of their life jackets by the surviving members. The huge shark was not hungry, but prey this easy was not to be left alone. Forty feet below the men it began swinging its tail back and forth, accelerating like a locomotive toward an Ensign with a broken arm named Don Harper.

The huge shark hurtled up to the surface slamming into Harper, jaws smashing down at waist level, lifting the man eight feet in the air, the enormous predator breaching a third of its body above the water, as the astonished cluster of battered sailors gaped, screamed and backed away in fright.

Patrick James Ryan

The shark came crashing down to a thunderous explosion of water, blood and lumps of Harper's tissue flying over a ten-foot radius from the brutal attack. The terrified men swam away, screaming at the nightmare vision of a monster beyond comprehension. The shark tore into the lifeless corpse of Don Harper and the ocean around the carnage turned bright red.

***

At 11:30 Booker and Chance were fighting hard to stay conscious. Dehydration and the elements were taking a heavy toll, as they began their fourth day in the ocean. Their faces looked like tomatoes, skin peeling badly from sun poisoning. Chance had three more episodes of delirium and Booker had to intervene to bring his friend back to reality. Now he was beginning to doubt his own sanity, seeing objects below the surface.

Twice he thought he saw a large, dark shape pass beneath them just below the water. Each time he rubbed his eyes, looking keenly at the location and nothing was there. A little before noon they heard a plane and doubted their own senses in lieu of the episodes of confusion. Sure enough, a little PV1 Ventura flew over their location. It did not signal, and it did not circle back to their extreme dismay. However, it did slow down and circle back over an area not quite beyond their line of vision. Turning around, it began to fly around in a circle.

"I think it spotted the main group." Booker said.

Chance was very weak, lifting his head up with great effort. "But they didn't see us, did they?"

"I don't know. Maybe not, but at least they're in the area."

"Yeah, maybe it'll come back."

An hour passed and the sun's heat intensified. Another hour passed and Chance thought he saw the plane again, but Booker corrected his delirious friend as he had done so many times the last twenty-four hours. The plane did not come back.

***

The monstrous Great White chomped down furiously on mid-shipman Ernie Butler, devouring the remaining leg and pelvis of the young man from Little Rock. Moments before Butler was jubilant amidst a group of twenty men, when the plane flew overhead and circled back. Cheering, shouting for joy, and hugging each other, they knew it would not be long before they were rescued.

A sharp tug on his right leg momentarily pulled Butler below the water. Rising he expected to return the hug on whichever one of his shipmates tugged on him. He turned expecting to see another over-exuberant fellow sailor, but was shocked to see a gigantic dorsal fin so tall he could not see past it. Realization sunk in and he felt the flow of blood from the femoral artery and a nub of bone just below the right knee. The men around Butler screamed and a second later he felt the massive jaws engulf his lower body. He felt like his hips were in a crushing vise, and the shark chomped down, splitting him in half, and Butler knew no more.

The big fish opened and closed its jaws below the surface, searching for any morsels of food left from

Butler's body. Several Remoras clung to its underbelly, parasites feasting on the chunks of tissue too small for the large predator. Temporarily satisfied, the great shark left the area and headed west.

***

Three and a half hours passed since Booker and Chance had seen the plane and both men were on the verge of a breakdown, where they could not think straight or speak clearly from the cumulative effect of severe dehydration and sun-poisoning. In the last ten minutes they had both seen an enormous shadow pass below the surface. Booker thought it was a Japanese submarine and Chance thought he was in high school again playing Ishmael in the school play of *Moby Dick,* only this shadow was dark instead of a glowing white. This puzzled Chance. *Why is the whale dark gray? Oh boy, this is all wrong. The decorating committee messed up. I need to tell Mrs. Dwyer. Moby Dick isn't dark gray!*

Chance was still fretting about the fallacies of the school play when Moby Dick came hurtling up from below, wrapping Booker in its mouth in a frenzy of teeth, blood and awesome power. The thunderous splash and resulting wave knocked Chance back several feet and he watched Booker being torn to pieces. *My goodness, this is way too violent. The ladies' PTA won't like all that blood, and the damned whale is gray! I have to tell Mrs. Dwyer.*

Forty-five minutes later Chance was adrift, alone, lips cracked and bleeding, imagining he was walking the hallway of Lincoln High School in Scottsbluff, Nebraska, searching for Mrs. Dwyer. The blisters on his face were cracked and oozing clear liquid. His tongue felt like a fluffy glove stuck in his mouth. The electrolytes in his system had reached a dangerous level, and death would be within the day if he was not rescued.

He never heard or saw the monster coming. One moment he was staring at the sky at a gull, wondering how it got into the school, and the next minute he was aloft, closer to the bird who for some reason squawked and flew away. A tremendous pressure hit his stomach and he consciously felt like he had to vomit and take a bowel movement at the same time, until his body exploded in a cascade of blood and tissue-filled chunks.

Satiated for the moment, the big shark dove below the oily black water, heading southwest.

***

Epilogue

May 1975
Off the Coast of Long Island

The two and a half ton, 25-foot Great White cruised the shore line off Montauk, New York. Like its slightly larger father, it was a rogue hunter, drifting alone from point to point, until the food supply ran out, or prey in another location seemed more lucrative. The food around Montauk did not stimulate the beast, or make it want to hunt, so it decided to explore some of the other shore lines along the coasts of Long Island and up to Martha's Vineyard in New England. Last evening it happened upon and devoured a slow swimming, defenseless prey, weighing 135 pounds, idling in the water about eighty yards from the beach. Prey seemed more abundant in this area, and if the food was this easy to catch, it would hang around for a while.

Around mid-morning it spotted a large yellow-bellied seal amidst some other creatures flailing close to the surf. The yellow-bellied seal lay motionless, flopping around on the surface. The huge shark swung its tail back and forth, and like a locomotive thrust itself up to the easy prey.

The Jupiter Chronicles

The sophisticated craft approached the previously uncharted, unvisited sphere-shaped planet. Blue light scattered over the atmosphere, giving it the appearance of an opaque, blue halo, roughly 257 miles from the surface. The planet had one prominent moon that was clearly visible with a second possible moon obscured from sight.

The captain looked at his crewmate in the spacious two occupant cabin and smiled. "How was your hyper sleep?"

"Fine, sir. And yours?"

"Good."

So what do you think, Science Officer?"

The junior colleague, shorter than his superior but equal in intelligence and esteem in the space program, smiled back, nodded and reached for an atmospheric recorder. They had been in flight exactly six months and a day on a special planetary exploration mission, eager to be the first to land on uncharted planets in the solar system. For the last two months, they had been engaged in extended sleep, while the craft was on cruise control.

"Sir, readings indicate the air is comprised of nitrogen, oxygen and argon with traces of water vapor and a host of less significant trace gases. Nothing that should deter further exploration with proper equipment and body suits."

The captain processed the report, pondering a decision. "Good…okay, we've got some decent intel from command center about this planet. I think it's time we separate theory from reality. Let's break atmosphere and see what landing options we have, if any, and what type of surface we are dealing with. By the way, how are you doing on the personal side? Miss your family….? How old is your son now?"

The science officer nodded, excited to finally be on the verge of fulfilling the purpose of the mission, while also lamenting the long time away from family. "Yes, my son just turned three and will soon be running all over the place! My wife will have her hands full! And you, Captain? Who do you miss?"

"I was never one for settling down with anyone. I guess this ship occupies most of my time. I get lonely sometimes, but right now I am determined to take back some useful data."

The science officer smiled, hesitant to tell his superior and friend that he should find a suitable companion.

The large spaceship cruised through the planet's atmosphere, jostled by the varying degrees of turbulence at intervals, as the two astronauts readied themselves both mentally and physically for orbit. Sensors lit up red warning lights, a cautionary admonishment that the hull was experiencing intense heat while the space ship rocketed through the stratosphere. Particle readings from thousands of rope shaped bristles made of steel on the outside of the ship detected the presence of dust and bacteria, alerting the science officer. "Sensors identified living bacteria and dust, Captain. The heat is disconcerting but we won't be in it long enough for any damage to the ship's exterior."

"Very good. I'm going to drop speed as we get closer to the next orbit layer. What do the long-distance, infrared cameras say about the climate's surface?"

"It appears this side of the planet is behind the large star, and darkness is making the surface difficult to see. There's a mixture of land masses, and I'm detecting a large aqueous area of undetermined depth, but dense and deep enough for a safe landing. The predominant composition of the aqueous body is hydrogen and oxygen with a heavy concentration of sodium and chloride. It's basically water, Sir, but somewhat different in concentration than the water we are accustomed to back home. "

"What's the temperature? We can't assume it's safe to land and release the watercraft, and we don't want to get vaporized."

"Yes, Sir. Let's see....readings indicate a suitable surface temperature, but we won't know for sure until we test it."

"Okay. Sounds manageable. Let's strap in and prepare for landing."

The large, sophisticated craft knifed through the bottom layers of the atmosphere, slowly descending on the body of water on the dark side of the planet. The two explorers were excited, flutters in their stomachs, and accelerated blood coursing through their veins. The ship broke through orbit, cascading toward the body of water and the two astronauts viewed the white caps and waves estimated to be around ten to fifteen feet high. There were no visible land masses in sight.

"Brace for the landing," the captain said.

The ship glided over the water three hundred and twenty-five feet overhead, descending at a rate of thirty feet per second. Five seconds passed….ten…..fifteen…..the ship smacked on the top of the water, hydroplaned airborne for several hundred yards, and slammed down on the water with a loud 'KUSH,' shaking the crew in their seats and knocking over a scanner, printer and interior table-top sensor.

"Congratulations on a successful landing, Sir."

The captain smirked. "So far, so good. We didn't crash. Grab the gear packs and let's open the hatch and see what's outside."

The water was slightly choppy, illuminated in spots like crystal from the light of the planet's moon, casting a myriad of shadows across its wake. The previously eager explorers approached the watercraft with a hint of trepidation that comes with uncertainty. What organisms lie below the waves that could be harmful? Are there poisons or toxins in the water? Are there living species in the water or on land that could pose a threat to them here or back home? Will they discover enough scientific findings to make their mission memorable and significant?

They started the watercraft and began cruising west based on navigational headers and a compass. A few tiny, winged creatures flew in the air, squawking either in protest or in interest at their presence. Sensors along the four sides of the rectangular craft picked up readings of a plethora of aquatic life of various shapes moving within a five-mile radius from their craft.

After forty-five minutes of gliding through the water at medium speed, they saw a land mass on the horizon through the light of the moon. Twenty minutes later they were able to see definitive shapes of shadowy land masses and glimmers of the topography lit up by the moon. Upon closer inspection a few minutes later, they detected numerous stalagmites ranging in height from low ground to small cylindrical hills equal to their height and even taller, lit up apparently by hot lava or some other heat source. They stared in awe at the lumpy, mountainous terrain, curious and excited to make landfall and begin taking samples and pictures.

"Interesting, Captain," the science officer observed.

"Yes, very. Let's stay alert for signs of danger as we explore."

They made landfall on a small stretch of sand barely long enough to anchor the watercraft, and hopped down on the ground. The first thing they noticed was the abundance of stalagmite formations looming ahead, as they cautiously began walking over the terrain. It only took a few paces and they came upon a diverse compendium of what appeared to be either some type of hive-like creatures or metallic-colored beetles scuttling about at their feet on a texture of ground that must have evolved from lava. Some of the creatures swerved in fear or turned around and went in the other direction at the site of the explorers, while others settled in and around the stalagmite structures to hide. It was impossible not to step on some of them.

Patrick James Ryan

"Looks like the planet has a history of volcanic activity based on the surface of the ground, but the haphazard and random configurations don't make sense," the science officer observed.

Let's get some samples and pictures," the captain stressed.

The science officer pulled out a Petri dish and bent down, scooping up one of the metallic-colored beetles, while the captain snapped pictures. The creature squirmed and its extremities swiveled back and forth in a rhythmic rotation as it had been placed in the dish. The captain took out a pick axe and began to chip some of the pieces away from an adjacent stalagmite, taking slivers and chunks into another Petri dish. Amidst the quest for samples, they noticed uneven patterns of light and noise coming from below on the ground.

"Do some of these creatures possess some type of electrical current?" the captain suggested to his colleague.

"It's quite possible, Sir. It is very odd and certainly worth collecting some samples to take back to command center for study when we get home."

The two explorers continued to navigate through the unusual terrain, gathering a host of moving creatures, pieces of indigenous rock, dozens of photographs and a variety of differing stalagmite samples. Twice they encountered some aggressive insects that approached them and spewed out something like a frog, only it was not a tongue and the tiny pellets that came out were detached. Fortunately, their thick suits protected them from injury and they simply stepped on the attacking creatures, crushing them underfoot.

On three occasions they unwittingly crushed some of the stalagmite formations that were more fragile than the more durable, solidly formed structures. At one point a large bird flew over their position at a fast speed, making them jump. It circled back one more time and they did not see it again.

Shortly after spending three hours exploring a ten-mile radius their backpacks were overflowing, and they decided they had gathered enough data and samples for a successful mission. It was time to head back to the spaceship.

"I'm pretty excited," the science officer said when they were getting back into the watercraft.

The captain smiled for the first time since making landfall. "Yes, our discoveries surpassed my expectations. Send the communication to the new base with the recommendation, with my complete confidence, that this planet is inhabitable and it is time to mobilize. I plan to lead a spaceship in the Armada, when we come back with a full fleet to colonize this planet. I'd like to have you again as my science officer."

"It would be an honor, Sir."

***

News reporters were gathered in the White House Press Room, waiting nervously for the president to come out to address the nation. It was 5:45 AM Eastern Standard Time and the fidgety journalists were like flies swarming at a county fair trash can on a sticky summer day. At 5:57 the president came out with a posse of staff and key cabinet members and took the podium. His face was grim and he looked tired, with dark circles having formed under his eyes.

"Good morning. Many of you heard reports a very unusual occurrence happened off the Atlantic coast a few hours ago, so I'll get right to it. Early today at approximately 2:13 AM the city of Charleston, South Carolina was attacked by an apparent alien invasion. Two eighty-foot tall creatures in large, black spacesuits came ashore off the coast. That's not a joke, and I do mean aliens from another unknown planet or moon in outer space. They destroyed eleven buildings and damaged dozens of others. They collected automobiles, people, and pieces of the buildings they destroyed and put them in large circular bins. We are estimating that there are at least two thousand people dead and thousands more injured. Local law enforcement did fire upon the creatures, but it had no effect. At this time my security council is reviewing pictures taken by people with cell phones and a couple of aerial shots from one of the F-16's we were able to scramble and get into the area. F-16's detected a spaceship located in the Atlantic Ocean about three hundred miles from Charleston and it launched back into outer space, before we were able to act. I will be meeting today with my Cabinet, the Joint Chiefs, national security advisers and key members of Congress regarding this horrific event. The people of Charleston need your prayers and support at this unprecedented time. We will have another press conference mid-morning. Thank you."

"Mr. President...Mr. President...Mr. President..." a stunned, jaw-hanging press echoed together as the Commander in Chief walked away from the podium.

Out of the Shadows

The president exited the room and walked into the Secretary of Defense, who had just arrived from California.

"I arrived as soon as I could after hearing about Charleston, Mr. President. I heard your speech from back here. How bad is it?"

The president put this head down. "Bob, I just lied to the press. The F-16s did engage the spaceship and fired on it over the ocean. Two F-16s fired all six of their air-to-air missiles and they bounced right off the alien craft."

"Our rockets 'bounced' off their craft?"

"That's right. And their spaceship shot back and two of our planes were vaporized.

"Vaporized, Sir?"

"I mean annihilated with one shot from their craft, as they approached orbit."

"Holy shit! What are we going to do?"

"We have four satellites orbiting Jupiter that have photographed what appears to be an armada of identical space crafts on the surface of the planet. The satellites have been monitoring activity for six months, but never detected any movement.

"Oh my God! How can we defend against this?"

"Bob, I don't know. I'm calling NATO, the UN, and the Russians to discuss the use of nukes. God help us."

A young, freckled-faced red-haired female aide rushed down the hall, pausing briefly to catch her breath. "Mr. President?"

"Yes, Elizabeth?"

Sir, we've received an urgent communication from NASA. One of our satellites just detected a massive alien military base on Mars. It must have been underground because it just showed up about an hour ago. There are several hundred spaceships like the one that landed last evening, plus approximately fifty that are double in size."

The president sighed. "Jesus Christ. Thank you, Elizabeth. Bob, order DEFCON ONE immediately and instruct NORAD to program target coordination to moving objects in the sky and stratosphere. Ground all commercial and military aircraft and get the Russian president on the phone." He sighed again. "Okay, let's see if nuclear weapons can stop these bastards!"

Hitchin' a Ride

The blistering, afternoon sun beat down on the pavement, scorching everything but the sparse cactus and tumbleweeds, randomly blowing across the road. The gangly young man with long, light-sandy-blond hair stomped his right foot in frustration on the berm of the highway. Unforeseen circumstances had stranded him without transportation.

His name was Ben McKnight and he thought he was going to pass out soon from the searing heat if one of the few cars that raced by occasionally on the lonely stretch of highway did not stop.

God damn it's hot! Probably die of heat stroke, he thought, wiping his brow with the sweat soaked sleeve of his black Blink 182 T-shirt. *Black T-shirt. Fuckin' brilliant, Ben! Genius! Hotter than hell out here and ya pick a black shirt, ya dumb ass! Jesus, what were you thinkin'?* He took a butterfly knife out of his back pocket, carried so he'd look tough, and flipped it nervously back and forth, pondering limited options in the oppressive heat.

Ben left Sacramento two days ago after heisting some coke from a local dealer and trying to convince his girlfriend, Julie, to come with him to Vegas. The ambitious intentions to sell the coke for blackjack money to play at the Bellagio started to unravel before they even got off the ground. Julie adamantly refused to go anywhere with him, while he was peddling that shit. After four hours of pleading and arguing, he gained zero traction in persuading her, and she promptly kicked him out. He told her to fuck off and stormed out of the Apartment with the immature confidence and swagger that only a twenty-year-old male can carry. He hopped in the car and had been on the road to Vegas ever since. Travel had been fairly smooth through California, with brief respites of sleep in the car, until the radiator started blowing smoke about an hour ago just east of the city of Barstow on a desolate stretch of the Mohave highway. Fighting a temperature well north of 100 degrees, Ben set out on foot hoping for a gas station or a rare car willing to give him a lift, as the miles ticked by. *Christ, why did I tell Julie to fuck off? Why was she such a bitch about the coke? It never bothered her before until that little skank, Emily, started taking her to those damned bible studies. Fuckin' cunt!* He kicked a rock that jittered along the gray pavement, slowly trickling to a stop, much like his 2006 Mazda when the radiator blew.

The sun pounded down and the noon hour passed, leading into the peak intensity of the mid-afternoon rays. Not a single car had gone by in ninety minutes. Ben's shirt and the top of his jeans around the waist were soaked with sweat, and thirst became consciously uncomfortable. Every other step seemed to bring on a wedgie and he constantly tugged at the back of the jeans to pull the soaked boxers out of his ass. He took out the butterfly knife again and began flipping it around. Another forty-five minutes ticked by and he was starting to get really worried, on the verge of panic, when the shadow of a vehicle caught his eye in the distance coming from the opposite direction. It slowly approached, revealing an old red rusty pickup, minus hub caps, closing in on Ben's stretch of the highway.

Please stop…Jesus, stop…..! C'mon…c'mon…stop!

To Ben's relief, the truck slowly stopped and he slipped the knife back in his pocket. A man about fifty with salt and pepper black hair rolled down the driver's side window, peering out at Ben.

"You okay, Sonny?"

Are you fuckin' kiddin' me? Sure, dude. I'm just taking a walk out here in the middle of fuckin' nowhere 'cause I like getting cooked in one hundred degree heat! Ben almost said. Instead he smiled and nodded. "Yeah, the radiator tanked on my Mazda a few miles back. I've been walking for a couple of hours. I could really use a lift."

The man studied Ben, looking him up and down with a bit of skepticism before reaching a decision. "You ain't one of them California faggots, are you?"

Ben bristled at the insinuation even though two close friends were gay. "Hell no, mister!"

The man paused, finally reaching a decision. "Okay. I guess I could take you as far as the next gas station and you can call a wrecker. There ain't no gas stations on this stretch for twenty miles in each direction though."

"Well, I would really appreciate it."

"Name's Bub, at least that's what all my friends call me."

"Okay. I'm Ben. Thanks, Bub!"

"Hop in!"

Ben ran across the street behind the pickup, noticing the interesting vanity license plate LOL666. *Old dude has a funny sense of humor. Laugh out loud and six, six, six. He's probably one of those old fuck metal rock head-*

bangers! He chuckled to himself getting in the truck on the passenger side.

"Did I miss something, young fella?" the man asked, sharp brown eyes seemingly piercing Ben's face with a powerful, penetrating gaze.

Ben paused, looking at the man, sheepishly. The old dude had been astute enough to catch a whiff of the private joke. Ben had underestimated his typecast opinion that the man was a country bumpkin. "Uh, no....your license plate made me grin. That's all."

"Oh that," the man shrugged. "What does it say?"

Ben looked at the man with a quizzical expression.

The man grimaced, thinking how strange it must sound not to know the plate, and recognizing the confusion he was causing in the young dirty blond-haired man's mind. "Oh…right. This ain't my truck. Borrowed it from a buddy," he laughed. "I have no idea what's on the plates! Good thing you're not a California Highway Patrol officer!"

Ben grinned again and began to relax, as Bub put the truck in drive and eased onto the highway.

"So, what's the plate say?" Bub asked.

"It says LOL666."

The man looked over at Ben with a remarkably young and unblemished face now that he was closer; five o' clock shadow beard stubble mostly black; sharp brown eyes seemingly endless, piercing and absorbing at the same time. "What does 'LOL' mean? A girl's name…? Linda…? Lois? I think my buddy had a Lois once."

Ben smiled at the man's naïveté, waffling back to his initial assessment of country bumpkin. "It could be a girl's name, Bub, but on the internet and in phone text messages it stands for 'laughing out loud'."

"Laughing out loud? What's that supposed to mean?" Bub shrugged.

"It's when you read something funny from a person online or in a text message that makes you laugh, so you tell 'em it was funny with "laugh out loud. You know? Lol.'"

The man shrugged again. "I must be getting old."

"Don't feel bad, Bub. It's kind of a kid thing."

"It's a crazy world…..so, where ya headin', Ben?"

"Vegas."

"Ah……Sin City. Been there many times myself. Never much liked it. A fool and his money shall soon be separated, or however that quote goes," Bub chuckled, with a twinkle in his eye.

Ben was about to respond and paused. Something about that last comment and a slight change in Bub's tone of voice bothered him. Bub did not look like a guy who'd frequented Vegas many times, nor did he give the aura of a philosopher, who would quote about a fool and money being parted. *Where in the hell did that come from? Weird!*

"So what were ya planning to do in Vegas?"

"Well, I was hoping to do a little gambling with my girlfriend, but we had a fight, so I'm goin' alone." *Jesus, why am I telling this guy this shit? It's none of his damn business!*

Bub's upper lip and right eyebrow curled up, a gesture that communicated knowledge and experience beyond his appearance and comportment. "Ah, women. Can't live with 'em, and can't shoot 'em either!" he chortled with a raucous laugh reminiscent of the hack of a long-term smoker, startling Ben.

The old truck rumbled down the highway. "You live around here, Bub?" Ben asked.

Patrick James Ryan

The corner of the older man's mouth curled up again and Ben began to dislike that expression. Ben noticed that not a drop of sweat could be found on Bub's body, but he was dripping like a pig from the intense heat and lack of air conditioning in the truck.

"I've been here for a while. I never like to settle in any one spot too long. Gets boring. I've lived in many places. How 'bout you, Ben? Where you from?"

"I was born in LA and my family moved to Sacramento when I was four."

"I've spent time in both. Sacramento was okay, but I found L.A. to be a cesspool. Too many assholes."

Ben laughed. "I know whatcha mean. Hey, what do you do, Bub?"

Bub turned and smiled and Ben noticed unusually perfect white teeth. "I herd cattle for my buddy."

"Oh, you work on a ranch?"

"You can call it that," Bub laughed.

"Why do you say that?" Ben probed.

"Well, herding cows and pigs can be difficult sometimes?"

"Why's that?" Ben asked, struggling to believe he was this engaged in a conversation about livestock.

Bub looked over at Ben with a split-second glimpse that made Ben think of the butterfly knife tucked away in his pocket, before the older man smiled. "Lemme just sum it up by sayin' the cows and pigs don't always want to cooperate, and sometimes it makes my job tough."

"I don't know squat about ranching," Ben said, hoping to change the subject.

Bub rolled his eyes. "It's not a career I'd recommend. It's kinda like when you got ten young people going to one of your rave parties. Everybody's spread out and dancin'. Well, when it's time to go home, you're the driver and you go to round everyone up. They're strewn all over the dance floor, movin' around all the time, music blasting. Some are in the toilet takin' a piss or shit or pukin' and some snuck off for a quick fuck with someone they just met. The cows and the pigs can be just like that." Bub opined with a mischievous smirk.

Ben stared at the older man, shifting uncomfortably in the seat, the knife handle pressing into his butt. *Where in the fuck did that come from? He's obviously spent some time in L.A. clubs.* "I never really thought of it like that, Bub."

The man grinned, showing off the row of milk-white teeth. "Hey, I bet you're pretty thirsty, Ben. Got some bottled water in the back if you want to reach around and grab some. I think the case is on the floor right behind you.

Ben spun around quickly for the opportunity to quench his pervasive thirst. "Hell yes, Bub. I'm frickin' parched." He grabbed a bottle, opened it and drank three fourths in less than fifteen seconds.

"Damn. Guess you were thirsty!"

"Man, I sure was. How do you not sweat Bub? I mean, it's hotter than hell outside and I can't stop drippin'!"

"Oh c'mon now, it ain't *that* hot, Ben. I guess I'm kinda used to it.

Ben nodded and noticed the water bottle in his hand was beginning to get blurry and he was suddenly very sleepy. He turned to look and was surprised to see three Bubs trying to talk to him.

"Rrrruuu allriiite?"

"Huh?" Ben asked.

"Iiiii seeeddd rrrrruuuu alllritttte?"

Bub's words did not connect, and in the back of Ben's mind, he was taken back to a time as a youth when he tried to talk underwater with a friend in a swimming pool. Delirious, he nodded and several seconds later slipped seamlessly into unconsciousness.

***

Ben woke to darkness, a throbbing headache, and sharp pains in his chest and buttocks. It took several moments for him to get his bearings back and remember the car trouble and subsequent lift from the man in the old red pick-up. *Jesus, is it nighttime? Where the fuck are we?*

"Welcome back, Ben. You must have been pretty tired," Bub said.

"How long was I out?" Ben asked, rubbing his eyes.

"Couple of hours."

Ben looked confused and a wave of uneasiness swept through his mind. "Why is it dark? Where are we? What about the gas station?"

Bub smiled and Ben swore he looked ten years younger than before the little nap. "There were no suitable gas stations to fix your car, so I took another road to a special place that can help you, Ben."

"Christ, what time is it and where are we?"

"It's still daytime out there. We're in a tunnel through a mountain in Nevada."

Ben's chest began to throb more intensely, worry and concern now full blown in his mind. "I don't remember any roads with tunnels anywhere on this route."

Bub's demeanor abruptly changed, brow furrowing, lips curling to a sneer, veins popping out in this neck. "Are you questioning me, Ben?" he asked softly.

The question hung in the air and it took several seconds for Ben to digest that the man had suddenly displayed an inkling of hostility in a menacing manner. His worry stepped up a notch to the first pangs of fear and he stuttered back, fumbling for words. "I....I...was....wasn't questioning you Bub."

"That's good, Ben, because I've got some questions for you."

Ben's eyes darted back and forth nervously from the dark road in the tunnel to Bub's face, trying to get a read on what brought about this abrupt change in the older man. "Questions? Like what?"

"Well, for one, Ben, when you were in the fifth grade at Kip Carson Elementary in Sacramento, you stole twenty dollars from Mrs. Schumacher's purse in the lunch room. Jimmy Zimmer got blamed for it and you let him take the fall. Did you know Jimmy committed suicide last November, Ben? He developed kleptomania after that little incident way back in the fifth grade; sort of a self-fulfilling prophesy you could say. After spending time in jail for petty thefts and shoplifting, he finally let the low self-esteem get the best of him."

Ben's mouth hung open in utter shock, heart beat rapidly, adrenaline shooting through his trunk. *What the fuck is going on here?* "How did you know about that? I never told anyone I stole that money! And you can't blame me for what happened to Zimmer. He was a little twerp and would have stolen anyway!"

"Oh, I know a lot about you, Ben….a lot! And poor Jimmy Zimmer was destined for a nicer life than being a thief."

What the fuck is this all about? "What are you, some kinda fuckin' mindreader? Are you some kinda relative of Zimmer's lookin' for money? 'Cause I don't have any!"

"Now there is no reason to get hostile, Ben, like you did back in your junior year of high school, when you, Arnie Kurtz, and Shane Swanson kicked and punched the crap out of Kevin Matthews behind the pool house at Stacy Donovan's house one late Saturday at a party."

Ben's eyes bulged and his sweat glands opened up like a crack in a dam. Perspiration stung his eyes and he wiped his face with the side of his shirt.

"Naughty boy, Ben. You broke poor Kevin's jaw and right cheek bone, and all because you saw him talking to Debbie Hershey in algebra class. You thought Debbie was *your* girl and she scratched your face a night later when you tried to force your hand up her sweater. Tsk, Tsk, Ben!"

Spittle frothed around Ben's mouth and he struggled to organize a response. "Look. I don't know how….I mean, I don't know where you got your information or why you're sayin' these crazy things!"

The older man continued to speak in a calm, controlled manner, knowing with certainty he had the upper hand. "Ben, you know I'm not making up these little snapshots of the past. They really happened just like last year, when you accidentally gave Mike Pisano a little too much crystal meth at a party down at

UCLA and he died from an overdose. That scar on your right arm is from where you scraped yourself on the rusty dumpster when you plopped Mike's body into the trash. How was it again that you told your other friends about Mike meetin' some bitch at UCLA and moving in with her on the spot to clear yourself, when the body was found ten days later? Oh, and you drove to the next county to get a tetanus shot too."

"IT WASN'T LIKE THAT! MIKE KEPT PUSHIN ME FOR MORE AND MORE METH AND TOOK IT HIMSELF!"

Bub smiled. "No need to yell, Ben. We're just having a little conversation."

"Look, Mister…Bub, or whatever the fuck your name is. Let me out of the car right now!"

Bub looked astounded. "Here in the tunnel, Ben? That just wouldn't be safe. Besides, you're in no condition to walk."

"What the fuck are you talkin' about, Asshole? Let me the fuck outta here RIGHT NOW!" Ben shouted, reaching around for the pocket to get the knife.

Bub laughed and shook his head, watching the younger man struggle to reach for the knife. "You have no knife, Ben. That fancy butterfly knife is long gone. Don't you remember?"

Ben's mind reeled and the first clues of his true activity the past day and a half began to filter into his mind. "Wha…what are you talking about?" he asked Bub in a much more subdued tone. The prior arrogance and cocky self-righteous attitude disappeared as quickly as the change in the direction of an errant leaf on a windy Fall day.

"You had a terrible argument with Julie over the drugs and she slapped you in the face and called you a loser. Do you remember what happened next?" Bub asked.

Ben's face froze, beads of sweat dripping down his cheeks, until the memory came back full force. "Oh my God! Jesus Christ, what did I do?" he wailed.

"You slapped her back, Ben, and she picked up a lamp and threw it at your chest. It hurt, didn't it? Because then you went into a rage and pulled that knife out of your pocket and thrust it right into her stomach, ripped the blade out, told her to fuck off and stormed out of the apartment."

"Oh my God!" Ben cried. "Why did I stab her?"

"You ran down the steps halfway to the first floor and collided with Spencer Douglas, who was just on his way to pay you a little visit. Spencer was not too pleased with the kilo of cocaine you stole from his basement when he started to reach for his gun, you stabbed him in the heart. He fell down the steps, awakening the old lady in 2C. You took off, Ben, and the knife was still in Spencer's chest, when you sped onto I-5."

Ben put his head in his hands and wept. "Who the fuck are you, m ister?"

"Oh, we'll get to that Ben. Do you remember what happened when your car broke down?"

Ben looked up pathetically into the older man's eyes. "Not really?"

"Think hard, Ben. What happened?"

The young teen looked out through the windshield, deep in thought. "I was speeding down the highway going about 105 when I came up on some old fuck that was only going about 55. I was pissed and slammed on the horn. The old fucker ignored me, so I decided to pass him." Ben's thoughts drifted back and his eyes glazed upward, and Bub knew Ben was back in the car in his mind, reliving the event.

"I decided to pass the old bastard. I knew I had time and no one is ever on that road. I know I took the turn and hit the accelerator around a bend. OH SHIT! THERE WAS A FUCKIN' TRUCK COMING? THERE'S A BIG FUCKIN' TRUCK COMING! FUCK! FUCK…! I swerved but it was too late. The truck clipped me."

Ben came out of the self-induced stupor and looked over at Bub, who was smiling. "Very good, Ben."

"What the hell is going on? Ben asked, disoriented and confused. His head throbbed and he raised his right hand to massage his temple and felt caked, congealing blood on his fingers. "What the fuck?" He looked down at his chest and saw a bloody rib poking through the black Blink 182 T- Shirt. "Jesus! Oh shit. What happened? What is going on?"

Bub smiled, but the charming milk-white teeth were gone, replaced with brown stained fangs with serrated edges like shark's teeth. He spoke in a raspy voice as if an abundance of phlegm was clogged deep down his throat. "You didn't survive the crash, Ben, and it's reckoning time now. Welcome to the taxi service of LOL666 - Legion of Lucifer and the number of the Beast! Let me formally introduce myself." Suddenly the truck was filled with flies buzzing all around and the man formerly called Bub laughed. "I am Beelzebub, chief lieutenant of Lucifer and I've been sent to help you answer for your sins!"

The tunnel abruptly expanded on both sides, morphing with a tremendous crunching of metal and rock and the road dipped downward, exposing a vast cavernous valley below, where flames and molten lava flowed. Ben looked and saw thousands of burning bodies with peeling flesh and exposed skeleton faces screaming in never-ending hellacious torment.

"So what do you think now?" the demon asked. "Not so cocky anymore you, little shithead!"

Ben looked over at the demon and gasped. The face no longer represented any semblance of human form, but rather a large, dark brown ogre-like face with deep pulsing veins had replaced the innocuous older man, and a horn protruded from its forehead with flecks of black and purple tissue caked around its base. A chorus of deep bass pitched gravelly voices screamed, "WELCOME TO HELL, MOTHER FUCKER!"

Ben screamed for five seconds before he was consumed in flames.

The Bunker

In the wee hours of the morning of June 6, 1944, along the coast of France on a beach strategically named Omaha, the sky was overcast and hinting rain. Waves crashed a metal-covered beach, slinking in and around obtrusive obstacles until receding back to the ocean.

A dark, insidious iniquity permeated the air like a silent, deadly, noxious gas. Though odorless, the aura of evil hung in the air, pulsing like a thick, lazy haze on a damp, humid summer day. There was a sense of powerful forces ready to merge in a cataclysmic confrontation, and tension and anxiety peaked.

Every two seconds, wicked bursts of 7.92-caliber bullets were heard from fifty round belts of a Maschinengewehr MG42 machine gun set deep in a concrete pill box, and showered down on transports in the surf like vicious metal hail pellets from hell. The bullets tore through the open space, knifing through waves and ripping through human bodies.

Like water flowing over the beach, wave after wave of soldiers clad in khaki uniforms hit the low tide beach amidst those whirling cylinders of death. The soldiers were comprised of young men from all walks of life, from big cities, small towns, farms, diverse religions, and every socioeconomic background, united in stopping the evil of Nazism.

The gunman imbedded in the bunker was hell-bent on destroying the invaders with a passion and dedication akin to a vocational calling, gleefully relishing each successful strike and kill, maniacally gripping the machine gun like a demented madman, almost orgasmic with zeal to kill.

Among the throng of men surviving the initial onslaught of gunfire on the transports, US Army Ranger Lieutenant Don Vickers and Sergeant Arnold Verhoff clung to the base of the metal abutments, trying to bury themselves in the sand to avoid the horrible swarm of bullets raining down from the bunker on the hill above them. The gunfire was so loud they could barely hear each other yelling two feet away.

Verhoff looked over at his Lieutenant. "JESUS, DON……WE CAN'T MOVE…! BASTARD'S NOT LETTIN' UP FOR A SECOND!"

Vickers grimaced, tugged at this helmet, and looked over at his shorter, lighter-complexioned friend who dispensed using the title of 'sir' with his blessing a long time ago. "I KNOW…! WE'RE LOSIN' A TON OF MEN….! TIM WALTERS JUST GOT HIT FOUR TIMES BEFORE HE HIT THE BEACH…..HE'S *DEAD*."

Verhoff's face fell, lower lip quivering. Tim Walters hailed from the same home town of Springfield, Illinois and the same high school Verhoff attended. They trained together and bunked together, when the ship left England to cross the channel to France. They shared stories about girlfriends, high school, and promised to keep in touch. Now he was *dead!* Verhoff felt a tear trickle down his right cheek, lamenting the sadness at the wasteful death of a friend, and mounting fear for his own safety. Walters would be the first of several friends killed that day.

The deadly bullets continued to whizz all around them.

Vickers, a rugged, tanned-skinned man quickly risked taking his helmet off to bandage a small cut over his right eye from a ricocheted bullet. Vicker's hair was a blond-crew cut and he had blue eyes. After slapping on the bandage, he took a quick glance up and gasped at a surreal snapshot of macabre carnage. The view in the distance was a look at the abyss in the deep recesses of that part of man's mind, where fear and the unimaginable become a living thing, a pulsing, palpable creature of gloom, despair and unyielding perturbation.

The water around them was tinged bloody red, reminding Vickers momentarily of what the Chicago River looks like on St. Patrick's Day, when town officials spill green dye in the water, but no one was celebrating today and the colored water came from the mangled bodies of his brethren. Corpses, torn to pieces from the barrage of gunfire, scattered the waves and beach like a haphazard pattern of leaves on an early Fall windy day. Mangled limbs, bloody intestines and innards collected sand, as bullets cascaded down in a torrent of blazing, angry fury. Vickers shivered and carefully turned to look at Verhoff, who was likewise scanning the slaughter on the beach. Verhoff's face was ashen, pale and absent of any semblance of its normal, youthful vigor, gazing at the brutal butchery of his colleagues.

Where the hell is the goddamned air support! Vickers thought. *Am I the highest rank alive on the beach right now? Fuck! We got to get up to the edge of that hill or that sonofabitch is gonna mow us all down!* A soldier stumbled past them, off balance, screaming, bullets tearing through his chest and legs. Arching his back unnaturally, the right leg was blown off from underneath, buckling the man into the sand. A whirl of six more bullets tore through the torso, neck and face. Headless, he was dead before hitting the sand.

Vickers looked at Verhoff and shook his head in anger. "LET'S GET THAT SONOFABITCH, DAMMIT!"

Verhoff nodded and looked up the hill at the bursts of metal still raining down on the beach. "GRENADES?" he yelled.

"NO GOOD! TOO FAR TO THROW FROM HERE."

Verhoff shook his head, stymied without any tangible options to move forward against the relentless gunfire.

***

The Nazi in the bunker swept the MG42 back and forth, honing in on the desperate men below. The murderous bullets continued to cascade down, tearing through men at a methodical, deadly pace with mounting casualties and the Nazi laughed, emitting a low, deep bass like chuckle at the spectacle below. The dozen or so men within view, who had not been shot, clamored to hide and take cover like the tall man and his shorter companion behind the metal abutment to the left of the bunker. The Nazi was frustrated the large protruding metal objects offered quarter for these men. His superiors placed the abutments in an effort to stymie beach landings. The Bunker Shooter's orders were clear, specific, and simple: shoot and kill everything that moves.

***

Vickers looked to his right and saw through the haze of gunfire and flying sand what looked like Roy Callahan, hunkering behind one of the metal abutments, roughly twenty-five feet away.

"ARNIE…ARNIE….ISN'T THAT CALLAHAN OVER THERE?" Vickers asked.

Verhoff cautiously looked over and shook his head in confirmation.

"HE'S GOT A M7 RIFLE-GRENADE LAUNCHER, RIGHT?" Vickers continued.

Verhoff nodded again.

"LET'S SEE IF WE CAN GET HIM TO SHOOT ONE INTO THE HILL UNDER THE BUNKER." Vickers said, taking charge with the assumption that all ranks above him lay dead on the beach.

Verhoff was still shoulder-to-shoulder with Vickers, and nodded again, instantly understanding the smoke and debris would provide several precious seconds to advance to the edge of the hill under cover.

Vickers carefully reached into his backpack and pulled out a water canteen. Verhoff nodded and gave a thumbs up sign until a bullet careened off the metal and grazed his forehead. The blow knocked him back on the sand just as Lou Rotollo scurried up from behind and flung himself down next to Verhoff, miraculously escaping injury and death from the hail of gun fire by inches.

"JESUS CHRIST! THIS IS BLOODY HELL! YOU ALL RIGHT?" Rotollo yelled into Verhoff's ear.

"YEAH, I THINK SO. JUST A SCRATCH….WHO ARE YOU?" Verhoff yelled back to Rotollo.

"ROTOLLO……29TH INFANTRY….I WAS ON TRANSPORT SIXTEEN…..THAT FUCKER'S REALLY POUNDING US!"

Verhoff wiped an angry line of blood on his head just above the left eye and shook his head. "NO SHIT! GOOD TO MEET YOU, ROTOLLO. YEAH, HE'S BEEN TEARING US UP! CHRIST, HOW CAN WE GET TO THAT PRICK?

Rotollo looked up at the bursting muzzle protruding from the slit in the concrete bunker and shook his head. "I DON'T KNOW….! WHO'S IN CHARGE HERE?"

Vickers looked at Rotollo, "I AM……HOW MANY SURVIVED FROM YOUR TRANSPORT?"

"DON'T KNOW, SIR…..BULLETS HIT US BEFORE WE LOWERED THE HATCH…..I WAS IN THE BACK AND ROLLED OVER THE SIDE INTO THE WATER."

Vickers shook his head in disgust and leaned back, accurately throwing the canteen across the twenty-five-foot divide between the two metal abutments. Miraculously the canteen remained unscathed by bullets, striking Roy Callahan in the shoulder, causing him to startle and fall against Bob Greene who was huddled next to him. *What the fuck!* Callahan thought, fearing he had been shot in the shoulder. After several seconds he noticed the canteen and finally made eye contact with Vickers, who was repeatedly going through the motions of loading a grenade launcher with his fingers, hands and arms, shooting it up toward the hill like a demented mime. Callahan stared for several not registering Vicker's intent until Vickers shrugged, putting his hands up in frustration. Bullets blazed down around them and Callahan shrugged back with a facial expression that conveyed, 'What the hell are you trying to say?'

Vickers finally mouthed and pointed to the bunker, "Shoot the grenade launcher…the grenade launcher….."

Callahan still looked dumbfounded.

Vickers was just about to give up when Callahan started nodding like a bobble head doll. Bullets whirred past and clanged against the metal. *He finally got it! Christ, I thought I was gonna have to draw a fuckin' picture.*

Positioning himself behind the abutment, Callahan leveraged the grenade launcher. It was a long shot, barely in range. He studied his aim for ten long, excruciating seconds and fired. The grenade just made it, hitting the side of the hill just below the right side of the bunker with an explosion of dirt, debris and smoke. If the hill had been any farther, it would have missed and fallen to the beach. Verhoff, Vickers, Callahan, Rotollo, Greene and several other Rangers sprang from the cover of the metal obstacles and ran desperately for the edge of the hill before the smoke cleared. Every second mattered as they scrambled for safety with painstaking anticipation before the sound and buzz of bullets slammed them from the bunker above. The sand compromised traction and they struggled to advance like children running in a shin-deep swimming pool. One of the other Rangers slipped just as the debris cloud cleared.

Enraged, the shooter in the bunker caught the movement in his peripheral vision and swiveled the machine gun to the left, casting a swirl of bullets that tore the faltering ranger to pieces, as he struggled to get up. The remaining six men reached the edge of the hill and flung themselves down under cover thirty feet below the bunker.

Bullets blazed down from above them at a forty-five-degree angle, cutting into more soldiers' bodies arriving on the transports and scrambling for cover on the beach. Callahan and Vickers risked a look back, slowly followed by the rest of the group, and the men gasped at the sight of their fellow soldiers being torn to pieces by the relentless juggernaut of hot lead.

"WE GOTTA GET THAT SONOFABITCH!" hissed brown-haired Bob Greene from Texas.

"YEAH, BUT HOW?" Verhoff responded, asking anyone within range of listening.

"WHEN I WAS ON THE TRANSPORT, IT LOOKED LIKE THE SLOPE OF THE HILL IS A LOT LOWER A COUPLE HUNDRED YARDS DOWN ON THE RIGHT." Rotollo said. "MAYBE WE CAN FLANK HIM AND COME UP BEHIND TO NAIL HIS ASS!"

A bullet whizzed past Rotollo's ear, causing him to lean forward, banging his head on the side of the hill. "HOLY SHIT....! WHERE DID THAT COME FROM?" he yelled.

"YOU OK?" Callahan asked while the others looked on with concern.

Rotollo nodded, face a shade paler than a moment before.

Vickers pointed to the right and then motioned with both hands for the men to lean into him. "THERE IS ANOTHER BUNKER CLOSE TO THIS ONE. IF THE SHOOTER'S IN RANGE, HE COULD EASILY MOW US DOWN ON THE LOWER LANDSCAPE...WE'D BE SITTING DUCKS," Vickers said.

"AND THERE'S PROBABLY SOME KRAUTS SET UP ON THE LOW HILL PROTECTING ACCESS TO THE BUNKERS, TOO," Verhoff said.

The men nodded at the valid points.

"I SAY WE GO FOR IT ANYWAY," Vickers said. "WE CAN'T JUST STAY HERE."

They all looked at each other with reluctant resignation, and the eight men slowly began to slink along the edge of the hill, cautiously looking for any signs of Germans as they approached the lower slope of the hill's terrain. Getting closer to the sharp decline in the topography around the bend in the hill, they saw the second bunker in the distance like a surreal déjà vu of their prior experience watching men on that stretch of beach get pummeled.

Suddenly bullets sputtered out from the low slope, ripping into Steve Reed, a tall, lanky Ohioan from the capital city of Columbus. He bled out quickly on the sand from a mortal bullet wound to the neck, severing arteries, spurting blood like a fountain.

"GET DOWN! Vickers yelled.

Two nests of three German soldiers, each sporting MG-34 machine guns, surrounded by a circular stack of white stones, opened fire up on the group of seven remaining men lying flat on their stomachs on the beach against the waist high lower slope of the hill that provided sparse cover.

"ARNIE, ROTOLLO?" Vickers yelled.
"YES SIR!" Rotollo shouted back.
"ON A COUNT OF THREE, LAY YOUR GUNS UP IN THE DIRECTION OF THOSE FOXHOLES...START BLASTING. CALLAHAN, WHEN THEY DO THAT.....GET UP QUICK...SEND SOME GRENADES UP THERE AT THOSE FUCKERS!"
"YES SIR!" Callahan said.
'OK. LET'S DO IT.....ONE....TWO......"
Bullets rained down into the dirt just above their heads and the three men tensed, simultaneously anxious to engage the enemy and terrified of being shot.
"THREE!"
Verhoff and Rotollo spun around and began shooting rapid bursts of gunfire in what they hoped was the direction of the foxholes. Callahan raised the grenade launcher he loaded thirty seconds ago and cautiously looked over the edge of the dirt embankment leading up the hill like a little kid peeking out over a window sill. The strategy worked as the Germans were hunkering down from the barrage of fire from Verhoff and Rotollo. Callahan looked quickly at Vickers and nodded confidently.
"GET READY, GENTLEMEN. WHEN HE LAUNCHES THE GRENADES, WE NEED TO GET OUR ASSES UP THERE FAST!" Vickers shouted.
Callahan's first shot landed square on the stones of the left foxhole, erupting a spray of metal shrapnel and stone fragments, killing two Germans and seriously wounding the third. Vickers, Rotollo, Verhoff and Greene were joined by Alan Park and

Tom Guthrie, and leaped up the hill, just as Callahan launched the second grenade up to the adjacent and slightly higher foxhole on the right. To Callahan's dismay the shot fell short, striking the dirt and clay two feet below the foxhole. Dirt and shrapnel sprayed up over the next foxhole, but the Nazis there were unharmed.

Rising up, the German soldiers in the second foxhole opened fire over the top of the stone border. Bob Greene heard a gasp and a gurgle, turning briefly to his left, taking in the bubbling spew of blood coming out of Tom Guthrie's neck like the flow of lava down the side of a volcano. Guthrie went down from the mortal wound, causing Callahan, who was bringing up the rear, to trip and fall, saving his life, as more machine gun bullets peppered the area.

Vickers and Verhoff zigzagged to the left of the foxhole, while Greene, Park and Rotollo went to the right, each group of men opening fire on the foxhole from different angles. Two of the Germans went down, the third readied something in his hand.

"WATCH OUT…..! GRENADE!" Vickers yelled, opening fire on the Nazi.

The grenade exploded between the groups of men, cascading shrapnel down on them in a malevolent, metal windstorm. A gnarled salad-bowl sized chunk of metal tore into Callahan's right thigh like an imbedded tic. Nasty threads of blood quickly darkened the khaki pants. He gasped and slumped to the ground, grabbing the leg.

Rotollo and Greene opened up with a brutal string of machine gun fire into the Nazi, shredding his uniform, while blood erupted from dozens of bullets ripping into the body as he flung his arms up into the air like an orchestra conductor and plummeted onto the machine gun tripod like a limp kitchen towel.

A small lump of shrapnel debris smacked into Park's helmet, denting the thin metal and making Park feel like he took a punch from heavy weight champ, Joe Louis. He staggered and fell back into Callahan who was just trying to get up again.

Vickers and Verhoff reached the first foxhole. Two of the Nazis lay bloodied and torn in shreds. The third was gasping for air with a bullet in the neck, lying on his side, struggling to get up. The weary American Rangers opened up with bursts of gunfire, bullets tearing into the man, making him convulse like a seizure disorder, until an untold number of bullets ripped into the body, spewing blood and viscera throughout the foxhole.

"TAKE THAT, ASSHOLE!" Vickers yelled in triumph and vindication.

The men looked down to the beach and saw a steady stream of hell still raining down on their peers. The sound of the machine gun was a bit quieter at this vantage point than on the beach, but they still had to shout to be heard.

"OK, LET'S GO GET THAT SONOFABITCH!" Vickers bellowed. The men all nodded and looked to their left at the bunker looming up in the distance.

"LET'S FAN OUT....FLANK THAT PRICK!" Vickers shouted. "LOOK OUT FOR MORE FOXHOLES....I'D BE STUNNED IF THERE AREN'T MORE AROUND THE PERIMETER."

Callahan moaned loud enough for Bob Greene to hear from a few feet away, blood now covering the left pant leg.

"HANG ON! CALLAHAN'S LEG'S BLEEDIN' LIKE A SIEVE....! WE GOTTA GET HIM A MEDIC!" Greene yelled.

"TAKE HIS BELT OFF AND TIE A TOURNIQUET ON THE THIGH AS TIGHT AS YOU CAN!" Vickers yelled. "HOPEFULLY A MEDIC WILL MAKE IT UP HERE."

Greene frowned and knelt down by the bleeding man, irritated that Vicker's response to the bleeding man bordered on indifference. Callahan shivered in a cold sweat and Greene scrambled to tie on the tourniquet while the others looked on.

"It's cold......I'm so cold." Callahan whispered, face beginning to turn pale.

"WHAT?" Greene asked, leaning in close to Callahan's face.

"It's so cold. I'm gonna die, aren't I?"

"NO, YOU'RE GONNA BE OKAY......YOUR SHOTS WERE GREAT....! YOU NAILED THOSE FUCKERS REAL GOOD!" Greene shouted.

Callahan smiled weakly, his face becoming extremely ghostlike, lips turning blue. Struggling to speak, he eked out, "It.... doesn't.....matter....." he gasped. "He's.....comin' for....us. Watch out! It's awful.....I..saw.....him...I...just...saw....him! He's comin'...."

"SAW WHO?" Greene asked. "SAW WHO?"

Callahan stared back without answering.

"HE'S GONE," Vickers said with disgust at yet another lost American life.

Greene shook his head. "NO...NO. I WAS JUST TALKIN' TO HIM!" he said with a confused expression.

Patrick James Ryan

"HE'S DEAD!" Vickers emphasized.

"WHAT DID HE SAY?" Rotollo asked.

Greene looked bewildered. "IT WAS WEIRD. HE SAID 'HE'S COMIN' FOR US' AND 'WATCH OUT."

Vickers frowned and Verhoff, Rotollo and Park quickly looked around in a circle, suddenly nervous.

"ALL RIGHT, LET'S STAY ON TASK……WE NEED TO GET GOIN' AND NAIL THAT FUCKER IN THE BUNKER," Vickers yelled. "GREENE, GRAB THE GRENADE LAUNCHER."

Greene frowned, taking one last look at the lifeless body of Roy Callahan and picked up the grenade launcher.

***

Up in the bunker Ernst Scheinlinger robotically moved the Maschinengewehr MG42 back and forth, mowing down the ever-increasing horde of men hitting the beach, and his mind began to wander back in time to more memorable, celebrated days of the past. He remembered the day in Berlin back in November of 1933 swearing allegiance to the Fuehrer until death, while being sworn in as a prestigious member of the Waffen SS. It was a glorious sunny day for the remembrance ceremony honoring the tenth anniversary of the Munich Putsch. He envisioned marching past the receiving line with dignitaries like Heinrich Himmler, Josef Goebbels, Herman Goring and a host of high-level generals and the Fuehrer himself in front of the Reichstag. *Oh, what a glorious day!*

Scheinlinger swelled with pride recalling the many accomplishments in occupied Poland after being promoted to command an Einsatzgruppen task force in 1941, overseeing the killing of thousands of Jewish men, women and children in the territory that eventually evolved into the Sobibor death camp. Scheinlinger smiled; a repugnant, grotesque gesture under the circumstances that offered no hint of mercy, an absence of any semblance of love, and devoid of any humanity. Instead the expression communicated a deep, nefarious, unadulterated evil.

During Operation Barbossa in 1942, he was critically wounded during the siege of Leningrad, losing his rank and taking many months to recover and restore strength from his injuries.

Demoted due to his limitations, Scheinlinger remained loyal to the cause of his Supreme Commander. Bearing down with greater intensity on the intrusive invaders, Scheinlinger was confident in his ability to contend with any assault they could bring. Looking through the scope, he noticed a man zigzagging across the beach with prominent nasal features, black hair, and a sloped forehead.

"Ficken Juden!" Scheinlinger said with disdain. He aimed and pulled the trigger. One hundred and forty feet down on the beach, Dominic Dimello, an American-born citizen of Italian descent, went down with bullets through his neck, chest and stomach.

***

While more Rangers like Dominic Dimello stormed the bloody section of Omaha Beach, encountering the murderous assault from the bunker,

Patrick James Ryan

Vickers, Verhoff, Rotollo, Park and Greene cautiously continued their flanking maneuver to get to the machine gunner. Rounding a corner ascending the hill they came across the first of two more foxhole nests en route to the bunker. Four Nazis occupied the first foxhole, completely unaware of the seething murderous anger about to be unleashed on them. The Rangers saw the thick, concrete-circumference formation, outlining the nest and four heads and torsos facing the opposite direction, and knew they had the element of complete surprise. The noise from the big gun in the bunker was much softer on this lower flanked hill.

"Okay…on three, blast those fuckers to hell!" Vickers hooted.

A copious measure of bullets tore through the four unsuspecting Nazis. Ripped flesh, flecks of grey uniform and blood flew about the foxhole, staining the cement and surrounding ground. Riddled with hot lead, each man absorbed over twenty bullets, as the Rangers used their weapons as extensions of their minds, releasing pent up anger through their machine guns. The killings were a catharsis, releasing the turmoil of boiling emotions, stress, fear, frustration, and revenge in response to the tumultuous experiences since landing on the beach.

The determined Americans passed the foxhole, Rotollo pausing to spit a ball of phlegm onto the bloody face of a young blond-haired German, as the group plowed their way further up the side of the hill to the bunker.

The second remaining foxhole lay adjacent sixty yards away from the concrete bunker. Much larger and sporting four machine guns on tripods, it housed seven Nazis spaced apart to detect enemy movement in all directions. Vickers paused and the men crept down on their knees to avoid detection, huddling close, hoping the Germans would not see them. The high decibel of gunfire from the bunker was lessened from this vantage point.

"This is goin' to be more difficult. Those pricks are dug in like 'coons in a corn field with guns everywhere." Vickers said. "Greene, bring that grenade launcher over to my right."

Greene brought Callahan's grenade launcher over to the right of the huddled group.

"Okay, I know we all got trained on this thing, but I'm not good with it. Who here's good using it?" Vickers asked.

Verhoff shook his head.

"Not me," Rotollo said.

Park shook his head, too, and all eyes turned to Greene, who smiled in a slightly self-deprecating way. "I can shoot it pretty good, at least good enough to hit them bastards," he said pointing in the direction of the Nazi foxhole.

Vickers smiled. "Okay. Good. Let's plan this out."

The men huddled around Vickers who continued, "All right. This is all new to me, too, guys. I'm open to ideas. Here's what I'm thinking. Let's crawl on our stomachs in a semi-circle roughly twenty feet apart. Once in place, Greene'll count to ten and volley two quick grenades in the foxhole. Then we'll open up on them while we storm their nest. It's about fifty, sixty yards, so we'll need to cover the ground quickly before the smoke goes away and they can see us. Since we'll be fanned out, we should be able to get them all.

Patrick James Ryan

Don't go too far. Let's form a half horseshoe. I don't want our crossfire killin' any of us! "

They all nodded experiencing a strange déjà vu, remembering Callahan's shots into the hill below the bunker a half hour ago.

"All right Greene. Do your stuff," Vickers commanded. "And be fast before those fucks see us!"

Greene quickly crept up the hill just enough to get a better vantage point on the foxhole. He saw the top of the heads of three Nazis, immediately worried one would stand up and discover them. Vickers, Verhoff, Park and Rotollo fanned out as planned. Lining up the grenade launcher Greene counted to ten and he volleyed two quick shots at the foxhole. The first grenade sailed high, landing about fifteen feet past the nest and Vickers cringed. The second grenade was spot on, lofting itself right into the center of the nest of Germans, spreading a wicked, solid potion of metal shrapnel, cement, and chunks of dirt, tearing into the seven Nazis.

The men rose and stormed the foxhole.

"YEAH! WAY TO GO, GREENE!" Rotollo yelled.

"GREAT SHOT," Verhoff cried.

Park nodded and Vickers gave Greene a quick thumbs up sign. "OKAY, LET'S GET UP THERE AND SHOOT ANYTHING THAT MOVES, A TWITCH, A BREATH, A FART. MAKE SURE THOSE PRICKS ARE DEAD!" Vickers shouted.

They ascended toward the foxhole like eager children coming down steps on Christmas morning, faces stern and minds bent on obliterating anything that moved. Four of the Germans were dead from a variety of head, neck, face and chest damage from the flying fragments of the blast. One sustained a leg injury and was crawling toward a rifle when Greene, the fastest of the men, reached the foxhole and splattered him with machine gun fire, killing him instantly with fifteen bullets tearing into his body. Rotollo arrived next followed closely by Vickers, Verhoff and Park in the rear, lugging the grenade launcher. Two of the Nazis gasped with labored breathing and the rangers opened fire in unison, ripping into both dead and barely living, until the bodies contained dozens of bullets. Blood, flesh, and torn tissue popped up into the air like sputtering sparks from a wood burning fireplace. At last after twenty seconds, Vickers ordered a halt to the deluge. The same emotional catharsis consumed the men, staring for several seconds at the carnage they had wrought.

Above the foxhole about fifty yards away, the side of the concrete bunker could be seen with intermittent bursts of gunfire spraying out each time the sniper panned back to the left. They stared at the bunker for several seconds with mutual knowledge of what had to be done next, yet a sweeping aura of trepidation and fear enveloped their minds. A palpable mental foreshadowing of something pernicious and dangerous hovered around the outskirts of their minds that they could not completely fathom.

Ever the leader, Vickers broke the silence. "Time to go. The longer we wait, the more of our brothers that bastard's gonna kill!"

"Hey, there's a flame thrower in here," Verhoff said, reaching down in the foxhole to inspect the weapon. "It took some bullets but looks undamaged."

Patrick James Ryan

"Take it!" Vickers said. "It may come in handy. All right guys, grab anything useful; weapons, ammo, water. We're closin' in. Let's go get that sonofabitch!"

***

Deep in the recess of the bunker, Ernst Scheinlinger dashed to grab another box of rounds, quickly loading the Maschinengewehr MG42 machine gun and resuming the merciless spray of bullets on the increasing swarm of men hitting the beach. He frowned, estimating for every invader he killed, three more stepped on the beach. Scheinlinger's commander advised him this would be a difficult assignment, but keeping faith in the cause was paramount and he would provide him with immeasurable strength, come what may. Scheinlinger knew from the sheer number of men storming the beach that he would eventually be flanked and confront the attackers face to face, invading the sanctity of the bunker. Then the real fun would begin. His face curled into a hideously profane smile, emitting a deep raspy chuckle that echoed off the cement walls in harmony with the gunfire.

***

The remaining path to the bunker appeared to lay unobstructed, now that the Rangers had killed the Germans in the foxholes. Vickers, Verhoff, Rotollo, Greene and Park crept quickly and cautiously toward the concrete pill box. The looming cement structure enlarged the closer they got. Like a beacon of doom, the cement block suddenly symbolized all the evils of

Nazism and their noble purpose and the Americans' destiny to confront it, pitting good versus evil in biblical proportions.

Within fifty feet they came upon a four-foot wide, six-foot deep trench in the ground leading to the bunker. Several German soldiers manned the trench, caught by surprise and gunned down by the Rangers. Four more Germans drinking coffee, standing ten feet above the grade of the trench by a Jeep adjacent to the rear of the bunker, jumped to get their rifles only to be quickly shot down by the determined Americans.

The Rangers paused as the echoes of their shots faded, replaced by the ever-constant rhythmic pounding of the big gun in the bunker. They could feel the vibrations of the big MG42 shake the ground in the trench, when they got within twenty feet of a narrow doorway leading inside. A gleam of sunshine split the door opening equally with shadow, offering evidence of another entrance from the opposite side on the east flank of the bunker.

"Verhoff, come with me. Let's find that other entrance," Vickers said. "Greene…you, and the other guys give us five minutes and then storm this entrance and blast that fucker. Use the flame thrower or the grenade launcher, if you need to. Whatever it takes. We'll cover the other entrance so the fucker can't escape."

Park, Rotollo and Greene nodded and readied themselves, creeping slowly and cautiously in the trench to the entrance of the west side of the bunker. Vickers and Verhoff quietly hopped out of the trench, crouched, and took off at a slow jog around the perimeter of the building. Halfway around the back they ran right into eight Germans sitting in a circle on the east side of the structure, assembling more Maschinengewehr MG42 machine guns. The opposing forces froze, stunned at the sudden awkwardness of being in such close quarters with the enemy. Verhoff could see a red pimple on the end of a German's nose, who could not have been a day over sixteen-years-old. The silence among the men was deafening in spite of the big gun in the bunker, which was muffled at the right rear of the concrete. Time seemed to freeze. Vickers heard Verhoff's stomach growl before all hell broke loose, and the Germans scattered for weapons, as the Rangers opened fire, blasting them to bits. The Germans did not have time to fire a single shot and Vickers and Verhoff cruised past eight tattered corpses.

Rounding a corner, they closed in on the east side entrance to the bunker, and saw another trench, identical to the one on the other side staffed with a half dozen Germans.

"Christ! How many more of these fuckers are there?" Verhoff muttered.

Vickers rolled his eyes and motioned for them to crouch down in order to sneak up on the trench. Fortunately, this group of Nazis, like their predecessors in the other foxholes, was complacent with the false pretense that nothing could get past the sniper in the bunker. It was a careless assumption that cost them their lives as Vickers and Verhoff rose up and unleashed a barrage of machine gun bullets, riddling their bodies with led.

When the sound of gunfire faded, it was replaced by a horrible high-pitched screaming, equally as loud and reverberating as the sniper's big machine gun, but the big gun had suddenly ceased fire. Vickers and

Verhoff froze, looking at each other with immediate concern and an inkling of fear. The awful screaming continued for another ten seconds and abruptly stopped. They slowly moved forward, holding their breath by the entrance to the bunker. The eeriness of the silence was incredibly unnerving, sucking away more of the taxed resolve that lay vested in the beleaguered men.

Carefully entering the bunker, it took the men a few seconds to react to the light differential. The floor looked very dark, in contrast to their expectation of the gray color of cement. The first thing they noticed once their eyes adjusted was a massive amount of blood that seemed to cover portions of every square foot of the concrete floor and a generous splatter on the walls and ceiling. On closer inspection, chunks of pink tissue, bone fragments and pieces of internal organs were co-mingled with the blood.

Vickers and Verhoff gasped simultaneously at the extreme blood bath, sweeping gazes over the bloody slaughter in utter shock. Vicker's stomach knotted and Verhoff fought bile rising in his throat. The gnawing question was whose blood was it?

A tunnel had been dug at the rear of the bunker leading down into a dirt floor with clay-covered walls cut into the hill. Sitting in a corner whimpering and crying incoherently was a hollow caricature of Ranger Lou Rotollo. The enemy was nowhere to be seen, nor were Alan Park or Bruce Greene present. The bloody massacre had to be the enemy's, Park's, Greene's, or both. Vickers and Verhoff feared the worst.

Vickers motioned across the room to Rotollo. "Rotollo, what happened?"

Rotollo just sat there unresponsive.

Verhoff took a step forward and his boot rattled against a small piece of aluminum. Reaching down, he picked up the bloody dog tags of Alan Park.

"Don, check this out......Park's dog tags," Verhoff said.

"Jesus!" Vickers said. "What the hell happened here?"

Verhoff shook his head in disgust and revulsion. "I don't know but this is bad, Don. What in the fuck are we dealing with?"

They stared in stunned silence around the room again. The blood was literally everywhere. *How could there be so much blood? What the hell happened here?* Vickers asked himself. "What the fuck happened here, Arnie?" he asked Verhoff. "This looks like a fuckin' slaughterhouse! Who could have done this? Is this all just from Park? Where the fuck is Greene? What happened to the sniper? "

"I don't know, Don. Maybe the sniper went back into the tunnel. He might be just waitin' for us."

"Then why didn't he kill Rotollo?" Vickers asked. "Something really weird is going on here!"

Vickers walked over to Rotollo crouched in the corner, hugging his knees to his chest, rocking back and forth on his bottom on the floor. "What happened, Rotollo?"

The deeply disturbed man stared at the wall as if Vickers and Verhoff were not even there.

"Rotollo....Rotollo..." The man sat there just staring and rocking back and forth. Frustrated, Vickers grabbed Rotollo's shoulders and shook him. "ROTOLLO!"

Rotollo opened his eyes wide, sporting a huge bruise and deep cut over the right eye they had not noticed before. Blood was trickling down the right side of his face onto the khaki jacket. Rotollo looked back and forth at Vickers and Verhoff, acknowledging their presence for the first time since entering the bunker. His voice quivered as he attempted to speak through intervals of gasping breath, snot dripping from his nose over his lips, rolling down his protruding chin.

"We......we...tried....to....shoot...it....We...really...did...We...must...have..hit..it....ten....times...but...it....kept....comin'."

Vickers and Verhoff looked at each other with mounting tension and concern, both thinking what in the hell Rotollo meant by "it." The horribly distraught man continued the terrifying account.

"It...knocked.....me.....in...the...face.....and..... shoved Greene...against...the...wall." He paused, breathing spasmodically and soaking in huge swabs of air with each breath, until he calmed down a little. "Then it just....it....it...it was so strong...oh, my God, it was just awful." He wept again, breathing rapidly and heavily again.

"What happened, Lou?" Vickers asked. "We need to know so we can get it and kill it."

Rotollo shook his head and waived his hand in a manner that communicated any action would be of little consequence. His demeanor was somewhat more horrifying than the blood bath around the bunker.

"Lou, just tell us what happened." Verhoff said with a softer, bedside manner than Vicker's."

Rotollo looked up at Verhoff and slowly the heavy breathing lessened again.

"Start from the beginning, Lou," Verhoff calmly asked.

Patrick James Ryan

Rotollo stared past his two fellow Rangers at the bloody wall behind them, reliving whatever diabolical episode that transpired in the room.

"When...we...went...in....the.....Nazi...sniper... was busy shootin'. Oh God...I don't think I can talk about it!"

"Try, Lou. Please," Vickers pleaded, kneeling down by the distraught man.

The traumatized man sighed. "I think he caught me in the corner of his eye......and turned. When I saw his face, I froze...oh, my God....his face.....I never got a shot off....his face..." Rotollo paused, tucking his chin into his chest.

"What else Lou?" Vickers asked as Verhoff knelt down beside the two men.

"He...was dressed....in a SS Storm Trooper's uniform....But it was all torn up. He.....he.... had a helmet on but the face was......was......oh, Jesus....the face was a......it was a skull with chunks of peeling, bloody skin stuck on the bone. Oh, Christ...! It opened its mouth and hissed at me...and I saw black teeth with squishy things moving around inside.....and the eyes, oh my God...the eyes! They were gone. Just the empty sockets in the skull. But inside there were flames...I swear to God there were flames in its eye sockets...it moved very quickly and swung an arm across my face....I....I...went down and it felt like a car was sitting on the right side of my head......Greene was dazed too, so the thing turned on Park, who was shooting at it, but.....but...... the bullets just seemed to get absorbed with no effect.....from where I sat on the floor I could see everything.......oh God, it was just horrible," he gasped for breath again.

"Take your time, Lou," Verhoff said.

Rotollo sucked in a big rush of air and continued. "It rushed over to Park and put its bloody, peeling hands on each side of his face…it growled and…..and…..twisted Parks' head away from his body. The blood came flying up like one of those champagne fountains you see at weddins'."

Rotollo paused and took another deep breath, looking down sheepishly, and looked around the room. Suddenly, his demeanor completely changed and he leaned in toward Vickers and Verhoff with a gesture that communicated he had a secret to share. Speaking softly, he said: "I know about that them fountains 'cause two summers ago my older sister, Connie, got married and they had one of them at the reception. I was too young to drink according to Ma, but I snuck in a few drinks. I was only seventeen then." He paused again, breathing heavily.

Verhoff looked at Vickers, who shook his head over Rotollo's macabre analogy. *He's lost it,* Vickers thought. Shots from below ricocheted off the cement block, and Vickers knew Rangers below were hammering the bunker, since the murderous assault had ceased.

Suddenly, Rotollo became animated again, chest puffing out, eyes bulging, rapid speech. "Then….then…the thing just……held Park up like a…a…rag doll with one hand….and….and…. used the other one to just….just…..tear into his body. It just fuckin' ripped into him…..and tore out pieces of flesh…..like…..like…..we'd tear up a feather pillow that got ripped open. Oh, God, it was horrible! The blood and body chunks just flew everywhere…I just sat there and screamed. The whole time the thing was doing it, it grunted....and spoke words....words in German...with a voice like a rattling car engine. It stopped all of a sudden, looking back at me and Greene and flung Park's body over its shoulder....and ran......it ran into the tunnel. Greene grabbed the flame thrower and ran in after it...I just sort of blacked out after that, I guess."

Vickers and Verhoff looked ashen, unsure of what to do next, minds reeling from Rotollo's story when suddenly loud screams came from the tunnel. The screams bounced off the clay walls, acoustically creating an echo so loud in the bunker it made Verhoff's ears ring. Rotollo's demeanor changed again, this time to a state near catatonic, curling up in the corner in a fetal position, shaking and crying again, murmuring unintelligible jibber jabber. Vickers moved over to the Maschinengewehr MG42, detaching the big gun from the tripod base and wrapping the long chain of .30 caliber rounds around his left arm.

The screaming from the tunnel finally stopped, replaced by the sound of bullets hitting the concrete bunker. Some of the bullets careened off the front, while others ricocheted off the narrow, shooting slit where the big gun had been just moments before. Verhoff reached into his backpack and stepped up to the slit opening, producing a flare gun, the agreed-upon signal to communicate capture of a bunker, and shot out a flare. A chorus of cheers rose up from the beach, releasing a collective relief that was palpable among the men.

"What the hell did you do that for?" Vickers asked Verhoff. "This bunker is not secured."

"Don, we can wait until the cavalry gets here," Verhoff said.

"What about Greene?" Vickers fired back.

"He's probably dead. You heard Rotollo describe what's in that tunnel. I'd just as soon not go in there!"

"You're afraid!"

"YOU BET YOUR ASS I AM!" Verhoff shouted angrily.

Vickers frowned and shook his head in obvious disappointment. "Well, I'm going in. I'm gonna nail that thing."

"Jesus Christ, Don, are you nuts? What are you trying to prove? Didn't you listen to Rotollo? Look at all this fuckin' blood! Whatever that thing is, it isn't a German. Some kind of a monster maybe. Don't do it, Don. Let it go. We can get the bomb engineers in here to blow the whole fuckin' bunker back to Berlin. Don't do it! It ain't worth it. Stop being so goddamn gung ho and think about this rationally."

Vickers lips curled up in frustration. "Are you finished, Arnie? Times wasting and Greene could still be alive. I'm gonna go in. If I sense any trouble, I'll get the fuck out fast."

Verhoff shook his head, slapped his friend on the back and Vickers turned around and went into the tunnel. After taking ten steps, the tunnel curved, taking Vickers to the left. A second later the entire tunnel closed, morphing the eight-foot high and six-foot wide opening into concrete seamlessly blending in with the walls of the bunker. Verhoff rushed up to the spot where the tunnel had been seconds before, pounding on the cement. "DON! DON!" His palms landed on something gooey and he noticed the cement was bloody. Pulling his hands away from the wall, he looked down and saw the sticky innards of an eyeball with the lens and retina still intact, staring up at him. He let out an uncharacteristically high-pitched scream like a little girl, and fell against the opposite wall crying and convulsing like Rotollo.

***

The tunnel was remarkably well lit and Vickers was unaware the path back out was now blocked, as he carefully weaved his way through the corridors of what was now turning out to be a fairly sophisticated labyrinth. The walls in the tunnel seeped condensation and the humidity rising to a soupy clamminess, increasing in intensity at every twist and turn in the cave-like structure. Sweat began to drip down Vicker's face and neck, drenching his shirt and uniform, as he paused to strip down to an olive-green tank top muscle shirt and khaki pants, discarding the helmet.

There was still no sign of Greene or the Nazi thing Rotollo described, and Vickers estimated he had progressed a good forty yards into the depths of the tunnel. Rounding corners and bends, he went deeper and deeper into the cavernous maw. The further he went, the hotter it got. The heat was now sweltering, sauna like as sweat glistened on the tanned skin, pouring off his body and dripping onto the dirt floor below. Vickers continued to move and the tunnel curved left, right, and left again until he saw an object reflecting off the clay walls lying in the middle of the dirt path twenty feet ahead. Approaching the object, he saw it was a severed arm and hand, detached at the elbow with a splintery stump of bloody bone protruding from the end. Vickers grimaced, muscles tensing, eyes racing back and forth in the tunnel for any signs of movement. He gripped the machine gun tighter to his body, trigger finger ready to unleash death on whatever lay ahead waiting for him. Copious amounts of sweat poured off his body, while he cautiously peeked around a wide corner, painfully slow, wired to the max for a sudden attack.

The tunnel opened into a circular cul-de-sac dead end, and Vickers gasped. Like the bunker, chunks of tissue littered the dirt floor throughout the area; blood puddles like gallons of dark red paint covered more floor than dirt. Flecks of skin, tissue and army uniform stuck to the walls in every direction as Vickers mouth dropped, taking in the bloody slaughter. Situated in the center of the cul-de-sac a few inches from the wall were the remnants of Greene's body. His legs were gone and something had shoved the flame thrower deep into the earth and impaled Greene's body on it, deep in the rectum up through the mouth. He had been disemboweled and the intestines were tightly wrapped around the torso, tied in a knot with a bow, holding Greene secure around the flame thrower. One side of Greene's face appeared to have been gnawed upon with deep red ridges and lacerations as if some type of wild animal mauled him next to the protruding tip of the flame thrower. Vickers stared into the lifeless eyes of his former colleague, noting the blood shot eyes and frozen expression of pain. Something moved out from the shadow of the wall to Vicker's left. Pivoting, he opened an eruption of machine gun fire, blasting hundreds of rounds into the shadow as it emerged. The rounds tore into the clay wall, carving out a wide swath of destruction, but they appeared to hit nothing but the wall.

Vickers waited for the smoke and debris to clear and a figure slowly took shape out of the cloud. Vickers gasped again, ready to fire another series of rounds when a low, gravelly chuckle was heard. The figure stepped out into the light and Vickers stomach turned, bile rising up in this throat.

The creature was dressed in a Nazi Waffen SS Storm Trooper's uniform with a helmet, adorning the snake-like insignia of the SS. Blood and tissue covered the front of the black uniform, pants, and black leather boots. The face was skeletal with shards of bloody flesh still stuck in spots, just as Rotollo described. The eyes were ablaze with perpetual flames and it was grinning at Vickers through blackened teeth with maggots and earthworms weaving through the lips, teeth and gums, making Vickers wretch and spew more bile onto the dirt floor. The Thing took another step forward and Vickers opened fire again. The bullets tore right through the creature, but it continued to advance.

"GET THE FUCK AWAY FROM ME!" Vickers yelled.

The creature's smile widened, revealing a bloated, purple tongue, while words sounding like someone was speaking with a mouthful of crackers emerged from the hideous face. "Now, Don, if I wanted you dead, you would already be dead!"

"What the fuck…? How do you know my……who are……what the fuck?"

The thing spoke perfect, eloquent English. "Yes, all of the above, Don. Your zeal to kill has brought you this far where the others did not have the resolve. We are so alike, Don. I used to be just like you, dedicated to the cause of the Fuehrer. Now I answer to a different commander and He's very special! But you are such a commanding specimen, Don. So full of leadership and vigor."

Vickers shook his head like a swimmer trying to shake water out of an ear. "What? Who are you?"

"Might be more appropriate to ask me who I was, Don, but we'll get to that. I am Ernst Scheinlinger, JD."

"JD?"

"Junior Demon, Don. You see, I have not yet fulfilled all of my requirements to earn my autonomy and sit at the left hand of my Lord and Master - Lucifer. My work here will enable me to enter the Kingdom of Hell."

Vickers felt as if he was going to faint. The heat was now at least one hundred degrees in the tunnel "What…? I don't understand?"

"In life I was a German soldier, Don, a member of the elite Waffen SS. I rose up through the ranks and was in charge of eradicating thousands of filthy Jews in Poland. I was doing quite well until an unfortunate accident claimed my earthly life, but I was born again through the power of the Master. You see, he looks very favorably on the cause of our great Fuehrer, so he enabled me to work under his divine guidance to wreak as much havoc, pain and suffering on you and your soldiers as possible."

Vickers shuddered, fighting the urge to flee, but mesmerized by the words of the demon.

"I think you are a smart soldier, Don. I could have ripped you to shreds, but do you know why you've been spared, when the others had to die?"

Vickers stared at the monstrosity, unable to speak.

"The Master has plans for you, Don, and you will not be given a choice in the matter. It's actually a great honor and I look forward to one day welcoming you as a brother."

Vickers took a step back and the monster advanced slowly.

"GET AWAY FROM ME, MOTHER FUCKER! GET AWAY!

The thing smiled and continued to slowly advance. "It is pointless to resist."

Vickers took one more step back and suddenly gathered up enough courage to flee. Spinning around, he took three quick steps and abruptly stopped in his tracks. The tunnel was gone, replaced by a gigantic cliff leading down into the depths of a huge chasm that seemed to have no end; a wide-open expanse into the abyss. Flames shot up every few seconds from deep recesses of the opening. Vickers screamed and turned back around. The creature was right on top of him, inches away from his face. Its breath smelled beyond anything Don could fathom, putrid, fetid and dead.

The creature embraced him with a grotesque hug. "The Master requires your soul, Don." Letting go of the petrified Ranger, the demon shoved Vickers into the bowels of Hell.

***

Epilogue
Bastonge, Belgium
December 1944

The German Panzer knifed through the forest on its way to the siege of Bastonge. The Germans were making a last, desperate attempt to corral the invading Americans and stop them with a vicious tank assault. Early reports indicated the Nazis were penetrating the American line, and all were hopeful they could keep the famed American General Patton at bay. Rushing through the snow at a maniacal speed, a tank commander pushed the large mechanized weapon toward the city in anticipation of killing more of the Supreme Commander's enemies who were pinned down. In the last several months, the tank commander had distinguished himself among his peers, displaying a unique vigor and zeal for killing. While visibly repugnant among fellow soldiers, sporting revolting third-degree burns and peeling flesh after his rebirth, he was fully functional and capable of performing all duties associated with the assignment. His name, Donald Vickers, Demon Fifth Class.

Patrick James Ryan

The Ripper Returns

London, April 1903

The knife flashed and glinted off the reflection from the dull toll lamp in the quaint living room, casting distracting glimmers of light amidst the shadows in the dimly lit room. The man gripped the blade with years of practiced ease like an old baker stroking and kneading dough. He loved the knife, nurtured and worshipped it. It was an extension of mind and body, akin to an extremity.

In stark contradiction to the pedantic, stodgy, puritan surroundings of the parochial decor, an animalistic sex act was transpiring in the middle of the room on the Persian rug that dominated the oak wood floor. The man, naked from the waist down, lay atop a naked, crying woman, who was begging for mercy from the assault. The vulgar man grunted, hips rocking back and forth against the prone girl, lying on her stomach. Repeatedly violating her, he periodically bit little superficial chunks of flesh from her back, shoulders, and buttocks, leaving teeth marks in the skin like he was nibbling on an apple. Minutes later after climaxing, he suddenly and viciously ripped the blade across one bare breast, slicing it off like a farmer sheering wool from a sheep. The woman shrieked a piercing scream of mortal terror that echoed off the dark mahogany walls.

Withdrawing the stiffened organ, the man studied the knife and licked the dripping blood from the blade while, the girl, still screaming tried to crawl across the floor to the adjacent study, lined with rows of book cases, leaving a blood trail from the sliced breast like snail slime on a sidewalk.

The man smiled a repulsive smirk like the curved beak of a vulture that conveyed both a vast abundance of experience and an iniquitous ambivalence. Snarling, he leaped on the woman, grabbing her neck, forcing her on her back. He began slicing her face, chest, stomach, and legs; relishing the deep red blood, drinking it, rubbing in it, and smothering his face in it. He continued the cutting long after the girl's protests ceased and the lifeless eyes stared up at the cedar support beams of the ceiling.

Focusing intently on her genitals, he made deep incisions, methodically carving out the uterus, bringing it up to drooling lips and chomping into the soft pink organ. He swallowed chunks of tissue like a crazed demon suckling nectar from the Gods. Breathing spasmodically, he experienced the familiar sensation of being driven by an external force outside his body and mind. Satiated, the scent and feel of the blood made him climax again over the girl's bloody torso, and he slumped down on her dead body, spent, ready to sleep amidst the bloody carcass like an infant in the womb.

***

Patrick James Ryan

London Metropolitan Police Captain, Michael Baldwin shrugged with exhaustion from the tumultuous events transpiring over the last four days, especially the past seven hours at the scene of a current murder. His tired mind tried to digest the strange twist the investigation had taken, leading his team from a dirty, rat infested brothel to the rustic four-acre cottage in the Waltham Forest borough overlooking the Epping Forest on the northeast side of the city.

The forty-one-year old Captain's physical presence dominated the back-door opening of the cottage. At six foot four, two hundred pounds of solid muscle, he was gifted with athletic genes, easily outrunning and out lifting men half his age. Well-tanned, with a few recent wrinkles weaving their way into his face, he took out his bill fold and looked at a family photo. He often took the picture out during times of duress studying his lovely wife, Molly, with the mesmerizing blue eyes and auburn hair, still supple and pretty after bearing three children, Colleen - a twelve-year-old mini replica of her mother, and boys Michael, age ten, and Patrick, age eight, who both had sandy-brown hair like their father. Baldwin was blessed in so many ways: a beautiful family, steady job in a noble profession, and harboring a servant's heart to right wrongs, and bring justice to the less fortunate and victims of crime. In addition to the highly noticeable physique, his unquestionable integrity and incorruptibility sadly made him both an anomaly and a pariah among many of his peers.

Baldwin stared across the lush green grass into the dense forest in the distance, reflecting on the long, troubling case that forced multiple inspectors into retirement or divorce, and haunted London for nearly two decades. Many of London's most brilliant criminal investigators worked the case back then. Men like Inspector Edmund Reid who initially led the case. Frederick Abberline, Henry Moore, and Walter Andrews, who were later sent from the Central Office at Scotland Yard to assist, all to no avail. Finally, Baldwin's close friend and former superior, Chief Inspector Donald Sutherland Swanson took over the entire case. Swanson retired from the force due to frustration and exhaustion in 1903, passing the baton to Baldwin. After twelve years Swanson feared there had been a resurgence of the most heinous series of crimes in his career, and he knew his heart could not take it. *Poor old Don. This shit would kill him to go through it again!* Baldwin thought of his former mentor and superior.

Baldwin had been one of hundreds of junior homicide inspectors in 1888 reporting to Swanson, when the wave of killings gripped London and introduced the world to Jack the Ripper. As sudden as the savage killings began, the Ripper fell off the face of the earth, leaving a terrified and utterly perplexed London to ponder the carnage and ramifications of the crimes. The stress and pressure of the investigation nearly killed Swanson and it took him many years to recover from the public scrutiny and mental strain associated with the case. In the Fall of 1901 when two prostitutes were brutally slain in Kensington to a precise exactness of the Ripper slayings in White Chapel in the late 1880's, Swanson had had enough and retired.

Patrick James Ryan

Baldwin walked back to the foyer to observe the team of officers scurrying about the first floor of the brick, Cape Cod cottage, gathering evidence, measuring blood splatters, examining the victim, and searching for answers and other miscellaneous clues. There was a profound sense of *déjà vu*, and Baldwin had been mentally connected to the emotional roller coaster of scenes like this seventeen times in the last sixteen months, and similar murders almost a dozen times a decade ago. Like its recent predecessors, this murder was messy, displaying blood in a wide swath around the corpse. The thick, red fluid covered walls, floor, and furniture. Also like the previous seventeen deaths, the victim was a young, attractive woman, robbed of a future, brutally slain, and left like a dead animal carcass in a field.

Unlike the original Ripper murders a decade ago, each of the current victims had been sexually assaulted in the vilest ways imaginable, with the killer sparing no orifice in the savage attacks. In spite of the profound similarities in all the murders, both former and current, like the excision of various organs, vaginal mutilation, facial disfigurement and disembowelment, Baldwin's detectives were divided about the perpetrator being the same man. The absence of direct sexual contact in the White Chapel murders in 1888-91, and the extended length of time between the series of murders, prompted many investigators to declare the current murders were being committed by a different person, or a copycat adding his own sexually twisted signature to the crimes.

Baldwin took extreme measures to bar the newspapers from vetting information about the current set of murders, and thus far the public had no inkling that Ripper-related crimes had resumed. After all, the prior murders gripped all of London in a paralyzing panic, and a return to the mindset of those forlorn days of despair was to be avoided at all costs.

Fortunately, each of the victims was either homeless, or came from humble means, making it rather easy to manage the ebb and flow of information. Baldwin shuddered occasionally, thinking about the media frenzy and public obsession that captivated London back in the late 1800's. *What would the reaction be now if people thought 'Jack' had returned?*

Baldwin shook his head, walked across the living room, into the study, and stood over the body of a man naked from the waist down covered in blood. The man lay perpendicular to the disemboweled, faceless woman in the living room, who was splayed on her back, spread-eagle, pelvis carved open like a butterflied steak, garnished by tendrils of intestines overlapping the mutilated stomach, thighs and legs. *Jesus Christ! What kind of a sick bastard does this?* Baldwin thought. Regardless of the number of times he'd witnessed scenes of the Ripper's killings, he could never quite fathom the brutal savagery required to commit acts of such a heinous nature.

He thought of the sliced-up girl discovered at the brothel just three days earlier and shivered in revulsion. There had to be some deep, dark motivation that lay deep in most deranged compartment of a man's mind, a part of the mind most people either don't touch, or inadvertently stumble across only to flee in fear, thinking something is wrong with them for even entertaining such vile thoughts. While acting upon them with such reckless abandon would be incomprehensible for any sane person.

The dead man appeared to be in his mid-forties, distinguished, well groomed, with a touch of gray bordering the temples and sideburns. The man was clearly dead, but in spite of all the blood, there were no discernible wounds at first glance, and the cause of death could not yet be determined until the coroner weighed in after the examination. Baldwin knew the man's name was Henry Redman, the principal suspect in the investigation.

The initial inclination in everyone's thoughts, including Baldwin, was that the deceased man was the Ripper, and had experienced a heart attack or stroke in the midst of the slaughter. *Are you the monster who has haunted my life all these years?* he asked, looking down at the corpse with a mixture of disdain and growing relief. Checking his watch, Baldwin barked at his men to be expeditious.

"Be sharp, lads. No dilly-dallying around. Assistant Commissioner Anderson himself will be here shortly for an update on the case."

A short, chubby detective named Paul Langford rushed up, flushed, sweating and breathing hard. The bangs of his stringy black hair clung to his brow. "Cap, we got something in the library. Found it behind some books on a shelf. Looks like some kind of diary or journal. You gotta come read it. I think it confirms we finally found our Ripper, sir!"

"Did you read it, Paul?" Baldwin asked, probing Langford for any hint of insight or perspective on the new evidence to determine if it really merited his review.

"I did, sir. He was a rather conceited bloke; likes to use big words and all that. I'd say he must have had a split personality. Pretty weird stuff in there, sir."

Baldwin nodded, feeling some anticipation and excitement and a short burst of adrenaline, tempered with skepticism over what could be a major breakthrough in the case. The adrenaline was fueled by all the chips of the crime scene falling into place, and the skepticism was well founded after hundreds of dead-end leads and theories on the Ripper.

"Okay Paul, let me have a look at it," Baldwin said.

The library was lined with dark mahogany baseboards set against a demure, beige stucco wall. A very large desk centered the room with an enormous floor to ceiling bookcase that covered the entire back wall. A candle with the scent of lilacs was lit on one end of the desk, burnt almost down to the nub. A roughed up, leather-bound journal lay on the edge of the desk. Baldwin sat down in the high-backed leather chair and picked up the journal. Reaching inside a jacket lapel pocket, he pulled out a pair of reading glasses, gently opened the leather cover, lifted the first page, seeing the telltale handwritten black ink from an imported American Waterman Fountain Pen, and began to read…..

***

I have never kept a personal diary before, regarding subjective memoirs as an eccentricity for the overly self-indulgent, but in light of the peculiar and insidious happenings the past six months in my neighborhood, I feel compelled to put pen to paper in the event an untimely demise should beset me, and supersede my opportunity to voice my profound suspicions to the proper authorities.

Additionally, I think a written document creates a permanent record and carries more credibility than verbal accounts, which often fall on deaf ears as I have found, much to my frustration, as I am mired in matters of life and death.

And no, I do not jest or hyperbolize. I am in earnest when stating what I believe may be an imminent threat on my life from a diabolical man who can only be regarded as an emissary from hell. I will try to chronicle events as they happened.

20 November 1902

My name is Henry Redman. I am a physician specializing in surgery of the stomach and gastrointestinal system. I have my own private practice, and primarily service the affluent aristocrats in London. The duties and details of my professional life are many and challenging, but I shant bore you with the mundane aspects of my vocation as they bear no relevance to the purpose of this account.

I really do not intend to sound so morbid and morose, but after you read what I have learned, I trust you will understand the exigency of the matter. You are well acquainted, of course, with the Jack the Ripper murders in the city just barely a decade ago. I was a younger resident at the London Hospital on White Chapel Road, close in proximity to so many of the killings that took place back then. I saw many of the victims brought into the hospital basement for examination by the coroner.

Let me state unequivocally that I have profound reasons to suspect the killings are still going on. I repeat, I strongly believe the killings are still going on. I also believe I know the person responsible for these slayings. Mind you, I have no direct proof and the police seem to think my ramblings have no merit, and question my lucidity on the matter. I know I am getting older, my memory is not what it used to be, and I have been afflicted the last fifteen years with migraine headaches that come and go without warning and offer considerable consequence to my well-being and equanimity. Notwithstanding this annoyance, I have enough clarity to strongly believe a neighborhood man named Edward Flynn is Jack the Ripper. How do I describe Flynn to you? He lives about a block down from my primary residence in a duplex apartment. Flynn is a loathsome, uncouth man with no manners or social graces whatsoever, a true vagabond. He is about my height and weight at 5'11, 175 pounds, hair a dark shade of brown worn over the collar compared to my sandy-brown short hair. He is handsome in a lecherous kind of way with penetrating blue eyes and a warm, seductive smile that I suspect touches carnal nerves in women.

Patrick James Ryan

The reason I feel I have some perspective on Flynn is somewhat personal. The mere fact that I am sharing my experience should lend credibility as it is a little embarrassing. You see, I am a bachelor and my professional duties eclipse any opportunity to date and court a woman. I have needs and urges as does any man, so I've developed an ongoing proclivity to frequent ladies of the evening. During these sessions I have cultivated a penchant for spanking women with a whip. I know what you may be thinking, but please let me assure you the spanks are more of a tap, and the women enjoy it. I never draw blood or hurt them.

I share this private vice because about a year ago I first noticed Flynn visiting the same establishment. He seemed to have a fetish for curvy, sultrier girls that oozed lust and sexuality, while I prefer more demure, Victorian women.

I ran into Flynn several times before a rather disturbing encounter took place about six months ago in the alley behind the brothel. I was just leaving after a rousing session with my favorite girl, Sylvia at 3:20 AM, a very late night for me, hours beyond my normal departure from the brothel. It was cold and the wind was blowing off the Thames on that frigid November night. Heavy fog was setting in, making visibility difficult, and the streets were completely devoid of people. I paused to tighten the scarf around my neck when, I heard a commotion down the alley. I turned and saw the vague silhouette of a man through the fog shaking a woman. A voice cried out, gasping, saying "Stop! Don't.....get off me!..."

Chivalry got the best of me and I began to walk toward the confrontation. "The clarity of the two figures increased the closer I approached. The man's back was to me and he was manhandling one of the girls from the brothel.

"Hey! You there! Leave that girl alone!" I yelled.

The man turned and snarled at me and I immediately recognized Flynn. He wore a ruffled white shirt, black vest, pants and coat with a black top hat. "Get outta here! Mind yer own business!"

"Help me, sir!" The blond-haired woman begged, with desperation and fear dominating her quaking voice. An angry red mark adorned her left cheek with the imprint of a large palm.

I tried to put a tough veneer on my face and lowered my voice an octave. "Let her go, you mongrel!"

Flynn sneered and flung the woman to the ground, reaching inside the vest to retrieve a long butcher's knife. The girl landed on the brick ground with a dull thud, banging the back of her head.

"Don't meddle in my affairs, Mister, or I'll carve you up!" Flynn hissed menacingly, waiving the blade back and forth at me.

I took a step back and he advanced, emboldened by my slight retreat. My eyes scanned the vicinity for anything to defend myself with and I saw a block of wood lying against the brick wall of the building. I rushed over to the wall and grabbed the wood.

Flynn looked me in the eye and then looked at the wood, which I was gripping like an American baseball player. He snarled again. "You're gonna be sorry for interfering! I'll get you for this!"

He lingered for another ten seconds, which seemed much longer with mounting tension, staring intently with a look of unadulterated hate, before turning and running down the alley into the fog of the night.

I rushed over to the girl and bent down. She was half conscious, an obvious victim of a mild concussion. "What is your name, young lady?"

She still looked groggy, but responded with a tiny smile. "Maggie. Maggie Campbell."

I helped Maggie to her feet and tried to hail a coach to take her to the hospital, but she ran away. Three hours later, I arrived home having no memory of what transpired during the time frame from helping the girl to how I got back home. I collapsed on the bed with one of my worst migraines ever. The pain was so intense I passed out, sleeping for fourteen hours, and when I awoke I was coated in sweat. I was deeply troubled and traumatized over the events from the previous evening and could only conclude the intensity of the encounter with Flynn brought on the migraine and black-out-spell. I knew I made a serious enemy and worried what he might do.

I staggered to the front porch to grab the copy of the Evening News and gasped when I read the headline and the short account of the murder, which I relay word for word below:

Local Girl Murdered!
I read the beginning of the article and fell back into my foyer, landing on my buttocks.
Local girl, Maggie Campbell was found knifed to death on the banks of the Thames early this morning. Police have no suspects and community leaders are already drawing similarities to the Jack the Ripper murders. Campbell worked as a clerk in the Metropolitan Library and is survived by her mother, Agnes Campbell.
I was sick the rest of the evening and stayed in bed.

Baldwin paused at the end of the journal entry, questions abound in his mind. *Blackouts and headaches. Well, that would explain a lot, but I don't know about a split personality. Who the hell is Edward Flynn? Why was I not advised Redman had mentioned him before? I remember Maggie Campbell! Christ, what a fucking mess!*

Baldwin's weary mind recalled the morning a fisherman stumbled across the remains of Maggie Campbell and the macabre spectacle waiting for his investigation team when they arrived on the scene.

The Campbell girl's throat had been cut very deep from her right ear to the carotid artery on the left side, a centimeter or two away from the left ear. The head was attached to the body by a thin umbilical width piece of cartilage, hanging by a thread. Baldwin worried that any movement of the body when the coroner arrived would detach the much heavier skull from the neck, and the head would bounce down on the ground or into the river. Her breasts had been carved off, stomach and bowels sliced open with innards hanging at various angles across the legs, and the vagina and all internal female organs were cut out and missing. Campbell's mouth was frozen in a horrified oval expression, flanked by blood-shot beckoning eyes that seemed to stare right into Baldwin's soul, accusing - *Where were you, Inspector? Why didn't you help me?*

Baldwin shuddered in memory of that horror and took off his glasses, rubbing his temples. They never found any clues on the death of Maggie Campbell. Baldwin put the glasses back on and read the next entry.

28 January 1903

Dreadful! Simply dreadful! My head is still pounding and I am very distraught over events the last two days.

It was shortly after 1:00 a.m. yesterday morning when I returned home, fatigued, and felt the first inklings of another severe migraine headache. Weary looking constables interrupted my dinner two nights ago at half past seven explaining that Lucy Kincaid, a rather impudent and conceited young girl residing two doors down with her dim-witted parents, had been found murdered. Lucy's parents, who of all things teach at the University, were traveling in India. Since I am regarded as one of the more reputable residents in the area, the constables asked me to go down to the station and identify the body.

What a dreadful business! The bloody corpse soaking the white sheet, especially in the middle of the body where her privates must have been located; the deep gash across the throat; lifeless eyes, frozen in horror, staring up at the sterile ceiling tiles in the police morgue all gave me a raging headache!

I immediately thought of Flynn and tried to relay my story about the evening of April 20 and the harrowing confrontation, but the stupid constable who was interviewing me, Paul Langford, was indifferent and kept asking me questions about my activities as a physician and how often I engaged the Kincaid girl in discussion and social interaction. Ridiculous! What a terrible waste of time! Langford made notes, thanked me and escorted me back upstairs to depart the station. I didn't get a chance to mention Flynn.

Then, just this morning.......

Baldwin smacked the edge of the desk with his fist. *Goddammit! He was right under our noses! How did we not see this?*

"Langford! Get in here!" he yelled to the living room.

Langford came rushing back into the study. "Yes, sir?"

Baldwin frowned and motioned to the chair next to the desk. "Sit down, Paul. What the hell was going on with this guy Redman? We had him down at one of our stations and you were interviewing him as far back as June of last year! What the hell happened?"

"Yes, sir. He was on one of many lists. You know he is a surgeon or was? Cut up people's bowels when they couldn't shit."

"That's wonderful, Paul, but why did we not do more investigation on him?" Baldwin asked sarcastically.

"I'll have to look at his file, but I think we ruled him out when one of the murders took place, when he was supposedly at the hospital performing a surgery."

"Come on, Paul. You know some of these murders are so ghastly with so much blood loss, it is very hard to tell when death occurred. I think we should have done more here. He was a doctor, for Christ's sake; he could have even done stuff to the bodies to alter body temperature and confuse timing of lividity and rigor mortis."

Langford put his head down, wounded by the rebuke from his superior.

"And who the hell is this Flynn?"

Langford popped up, relieved for the chance to share accurate information. "Flynn is a former police officer. He was in Ireland originally and had experience with some serial killings of women there in the early 1880's. When he moved to England, Scotland Yard learned about him from his superiors in Ireland, and he assisted us in the first couple of Jack murders back in 1888. He's a private investigator now."

"Did you know Redman thought Flynn was the Ripper?" Baldwin asked.

Langford shook his head. "Redman was crazy, Sir. Keep reading the diary."

Baldwin studied Langford's face for a few seconds, searching for any twitch or sign of uncertainty in his resolve about Redman. "Well, I will say the man's writing is paranoid delusional at times and narcissistic. Too bad we can't interview him now, since he's dead! Dammit!"

"He's our boy, sir." Langford stated, looking down at his feet, embarrassed that Baldwin never saw Redman's file.

Baldwin shook his head. "Let's not be premature, Paul. Time will tell. If there are no more murders, he's *probably* our boy....you better go back out to the body and other detectives now. Thanks, Paul." Langford left the study and Baldwin returned to the strange journal of Dr. Henry Redman.

......I took the day off and was walking around town to handle some errands when I caught Flynn following me. After dropping a suit at the tailors, I saw him lurking in the door front of the bakery across the street. He made no effort to be covert or conceal his intent, but rather openly stared with copious antipathy and ambivalence.

Ten minutes later, I spotted him in the bank lobby when making a cash withdrawal. He sneered and took stiffened fingers across his neck, a gesture meant for me leaving no question about his evil intentions. I walked over to the constable assigned to the bank, but by the time I brought him over to the lobby, Flynn was gone.

An hour after the bank incident I was leaving my personal physician's office with yet another proposed remedy for the headaches and blackout spells, when I bumped into Flynn rounding a corner to the alley. Our shoulders banged and he snarled at me like a rabid dog.

"I told you I'm gonna get you, you meddler!"

I was in shock and just stood there a foot away from this maniacal monster. Spittle frothed at his mouth, sticking on the whiskers that had not been shaved for several days.

"I know all about you." Flynn seethed like a snake. "You posture yourself like some pillar of the community; the benevolent doctor. What a façade!" Flynn mocked. "I've fucked some of the same girls you've fucked at that trashy whorehouse. I know what you like to do to them. I know everything you do and it's gonna catch up to you because I'm going to get you. You're not gonna get away with what you are doing! Remember, I'm watching you and you better quit telling lies about me and watch yourself!"

I stood there shaking and perplexed in the alley, digesting the tapestry of words spewed by Flynn against my character.

As I reflect on it now as I pen this, I ask myself how did he know about the little games I play with the girls down at Madame Amy's House? He must know that I have been watching him and have tried to discuss him with the police. But how? He has decided to dedicate himself to my ruin and is coming after me!

I am at a loss for words and I'm going to take one of my doctor's new pills and go to bed!

Baldwin put the journal down and called for Officer Langford a second time. "Paul! Get in here again!"

Langford rushed in from the living room, sweating and looking haggard.

"What's wrong with you?" Baldwin asked exasperated.

"The coroner arrived and we've been trying to lift the bodies up in place so he can look over them. They're heavy as hell, sir!"

"Yeah, I saw him pull up. Get some of the younger junior deputies to lift them. You're going to have a heart attack."

Langford wiped sweat from his brow and stood nervously waiting for what Baldwin called him in to discuss.

"Well, sit down and relax a minute; I've got another question," Baldwin said waving his hand toward a chair. "Did Redman tell you in your conversations with him that he thought Flynn was tailing him?"

"I believe he did sir, but we didn't give it much stock, because Flynn had access to the case files from the former work back in 1888. We just assumed he was keeping a watchful eye on Redman, since they lived catty-corner to each other in the same neighborhood. He must have known Redman was once a suspect."

Baldwin slowly nodded and shook his head. "There is something not quite right about all of this, but I can't figure it out. Redman sounds like a paranoid schizo in this journal, but the commiserating with the prostitutes fits with the Ripper. The headaches and blackout spells fit with someone having a potential alter ego, or split personality, hidden and disguised to the public persona until committing the crimes...."

Baldwin frowned, pausing for a few seconds in deep thought. "But after all this time, Paul, and all the hundreds of leads trying to get the Ripper, it's just all a little too convenient today. I almost feel like Redman has been gift wrapped for us."

"He did by admission in the journal have contact with several of the victims and he is covered in this victim's blood." Langford countered.

"I know…..maybe I'm just grasping at straws, Paul. I still have a couple more pages to read in this thing. Hang close in case I need you again."

Langford nodded and went back into the living room with a host of his cohorts and the coroner who was busy making notes, ordering everyone around. Baldwin picked up the journal and continued with the next entry.

20 March 1903

I am trying to write now before the headaches return. Oh, I am so upset, just beside myself. It is so very dreadful. I am so confused. I have been looking out the window the last three hours since I woke up, fearing a visit from the police. Oh my God, where do I begin?

Last night I went to the brothel I frequent a couple times a week for some female attention to reduce all the stress from this Flynn business. Unfortunately, Sylvia was not well and I had to settle for a skinny girl named Liz, who looked like she was barely a day over twelve. In spite of appearances, Liz was well versed on the needs of men, dropping the demure persona in conjunction with the loss of her clothes. She proved to be quite adept at serving my special requests. I think she took me to climax three times as the hours melted away, and I found myself dozing off, head tucked comfortably against her naked breasts.

The light dozing must have turned into full-fledged sleep because I woke up much later feeling wetness against my cheek along with the thick, pungent odor of copper that instantly reminded me of the operating room. I sat up in the bed and turned the light on to a nightmare beyond any realm of my imagination.

I immediately gagged and spewed vomit on the pillow. Liz lay next to me, cut to pieces. Her decapitated head was on the pillar of the headboard; chest and stomach sliced open with internal organs spilling about like the tentacles of an octopus. Her breasts were gone and all that remained were two oval shaped holes in the chest cavity where my head lay moments before. She was lying on her back, spread eagled and all the flesh from her inner thighs up to the top of the pelvis bone had been carved out.

I retched again as I noticed the insignia of a pentagram carved into the soft flesh of her right inner thigh. A rush of crazy questions shot through my mind. What the hell? Who the hell did this? Why did I not hear anything? I tried to stand up, a wave of dizziness hitting me hard, and I noticed my naked body was covered in blood. I tripped on some of my clothing, hitting the floor hard and passed out again. I don't have any idea how long I was out, but I was awakened by pounding on the door. It was the house Madame, Marie, telling me time was up and I had to leave or she would call the police.

"I've been trying to reach you for hours now, Mr. Redman! Time is up. It's 4:00 AM and we are shutting down for the night. What is going on in there? Let me in right now!"

I had no intention of letting her in, of course. How would I explain? I had to get out of there! Scrambling for clothing as Marie continued to knock on the door, I rushed over to the window and made my way down the fire escape and took off running. I did not stop until I burst into the door of the house and fell against the wood floor of the foyer. I passed out again until I was awakened by the noon sun coming in through the east window. My head throbbed then, and it is throbbing again now. I must stop and rest and I'll finish this entry later.

"Jesus Christ!" Baldwin quipped out loud in the library. "He's the damned Ripper and doesn't even know it!" He flipped the page like an eager teenager reading a forbidden, adult erotica column, excited to read the next words from Henry Redman.

The nap did not help as I could only toss and turn, pondering the myriad of possible explanations for what happened that culminated into the murder, and torturing myself with the nightmarish, horrific visions of the girl's butchered body.

My mind reeled back and forth. Could Flynn have slipped in and somehow drugged me and committed the crime? Surely someone would have heard him?

I just had another thought hit me! What if I am actually committing these heinous murders and cannot remember? Oh my God! What if it is me? The Madame and several of her employees saw me with poor Liz. They have undoubtedly talked to the police. It's just a matter of time before they arrive. They will never believe me about Flynn. I've got to get out of here. I have to have time to think on this and figure out what happened. I will go to the summer cottage to get my wits about me and add future journal entries, when I have a calmer state of mind.

I can't remember anything beyond the love making with the girl. Jesus, why can't I remember? It had to be that diabolical Flynn. If something happens to me before I have a chance to speak to proper authorities, I trust this record will aid in the truth being revealed.

Baldwin paused at the end of the page, flipping it over, disappointed Redman made no further entries. He took the glasses off and rubbed his temples. *Well, Dr. Redman, I think you shed plenty of truth on the matter. I wonder if you even consciously knew what you were doing.*

He took out his wallet again and looked at pictures of his wife, Molly, and mother, Catherine, women he revered, loved and respected. Baldwin lamented with a mixture of sadness. *How could anyone denigrate and destroy women in such an evil, heinous fashion?* It appeared that the long-awaited closure to the whole Ripper saga was finally at hand. Sighing, he heard a knock on the door to the library.

"Yes?"

"Sir, Langford here again. We've got Edward Flynn outside. We picked him up so you could question him."

Baldwin sighed again, deeply. "Okay....send him in the side door away from the crime scene. There are a couple of loose ends I'd like to wrap up. I want you to sit in, too, Paul."

"Yes, sir. I was going to suggest we come in through the back door to avoid the mess out front."

"Even better," Baldwin responded.

Five minutes later Langford escorted a middle-aged man of average height, well built, with brown hair in need of a cut, lying just slightly over the collar. Fitting Redman's description in the journal, Flynn was unshaven, and in spite of the slightly gruff appearance, he donned a business suit and was blessed with handsome facial features and prominent blue eyes. He had the demeanor of someone instantly likable by most people and would universally be considered attractive.

"Captain Baldwin?" Flynn asked, extending his hand.

"Yes and you are Inspector Edward Flynn?"

Flynn smiled at the reference to the former life of police work. "Retired Inspector, Captain."

"Yes, Langford here tells me you're originally from Ireland and came to us when the first series of Jack killings took place?"

"That is partly correct. I worked at a distance on a series of murders in County Cork, when I was still working as a police officer on several cases that had some eerie similarities to your Ripper killings. I am originally from County Kerry and the Cork police force was very short on staff, so my Captain volunteered me to assist. However, I was not detailed very long as I came to London to tend to an ailing aunt who passed away roughly six months prior to your Ripper. In fact, I still live in her house, as I was her only heir."

Baldwin nodded. "That makes sense. I wasn't privy to the particulars and knew Scotland Yard reached out to you in 1889…thought it was for some help with Jack. What would you say the similarities are between your Irish serial killer and our Jack the Ripper?"

Flynn frowned and sat down across the desk from Baldwin. "The women in Ireland all were vaginally mutilated, very bloody and messy every time, with wanton debauchery and despicable acts perpetrated on their bodies. Sounds pretty similar to what your man, Langford described here."

Baldwin took note of the emphasis Flynn placed on the word 'despicable' making it sound like the hiss of a snake.

"Did you ever have any solid leads?"

Flynn shook his head. "Never….oh, some of the locals had some crazy theories on this person or that person. One even swore it was a local parish priest, but every lead ended up a dead end."

Baldwin studied Flynn, recognizing the usual police jargon and began to relax, knowing the most important question had yet to be asked. "You know, Mr. Flynn, Henry Redman's diary mentions you several times throughout each entry, some of which are not very flattering."

Flynn smiled and rolled his eyes. "I'm not surprised. He lived close to the duplex I inherited from my aunt and the neighborhood knew of his......" Flynn paused, rubbing the index finger and thumb of his right hand across the stubble of his chin, pondering words. "Shall we say.....perverse sexual practices. I suppose when I ran into him, I may have looked at him with a little too much scrutiny. The old police officer in me always suspected something was wrong with the peculiar doctor."

Baldwin nodded. The word *peculiar* described Redman perfectly.

Flynn continued. "I saw him one evening near the Thames when taking a walk. He was roughing up a blond-haired woman and I tried to intervene. He cursed and called me some crazy names, before picking up a large block of wood and threatening me. I did not get a very good look at the girl, but she was on her knees and crying, and I had to flee before he attacked me. I reported that to Detective Langford," Flynn said, looking up at the chubby officer."

Langford nodded.

Baldwin looked at Langford, knowing they both were thinking of Redman's description in the diary of the encounter with Maggie Campbell.

"After that, I saw him one more time and warned him that I knew what he was doing to women, and I would see to it that justice was done. I was probably overstepping my bounds, but I wanted to rattle him a little bit and just see how he would react."

"What did he say when you called him out?" Baldwin asked.

"Well, it was brief. I had some banking to do when we ran into each other, simultaneously leaving tellers after drawing out some money. We bumped into each other and he seemed to be surprised, so I seized the moment to challenge him."

Flynn paused, smiling and shaking his head. "Captain, he just stared at me and did not say a word after I said my peace. It was very strange."

Baldwin took a few notes and looked back up at the former Irish cop. "I appreciate you coming here on such short notice. Please keep all of this under wraps for now for obvious reasons."

Flynn smiled grimly. "Of course."

"If you think of anything else, please contact us."

The men shook hands and Langford escorted Edward Flynn out. Ten minutes later Assistant Commissioner Anderson arrived, entering through the back door, and Baldwin relayed what they had discovered to the distinguished older gentleman, emphasizing that it was a strong likelihood they finally solved the mystery of Jack the Ripper. As Baldwin suspected, Anderson immediately ordered that the investigation and its conclusions be buried for the sake of all parties involved. London and the world would be better off and confidence in the police would be forever compromised, if they knew another series of grisly murders hit the city. Baldwin frowned and followed Anderson into the bloody crime scene in the living room.

Epilogue
May 5, 1903

The big ship cruised steadily through the ocean, seamlessly knifing through the waves at an even eight knots, departing from Liverpool, England four hours ago en route to Boston, Massachusetts in America. A full moon lit up the port bow, illuminating the deck and the diverse group of passengers milling about at half past 9:00 in the evening. They were enjoying casual conversation and the light breeze coming from the west across the Northern Hemisphere.

A ruggedly handsome man with brown hair clad in a grey suit and red tie paused to light a cigarette, studying the many attractive, wealthy women situated near him in first class on the RMS *Carpathia,* a new ship on her maiden voyage across the Atlantic. Some of the women were paired with their married husbands; others were younger teens walking with parents, and an occasional pair of sisters walked together unaccompanied by a man. Most noticed the strikingly handsome gentleman smoking the cigarette against the railing. The man smiled at the subtle, barely detectable, unconscious signals of sexual interest from the women. He was excited about the abundant opportunities that lay waiting for him in America. He leaned against a railing completely confident his true demonic identify would never be revealed to the human prey.

The handsome demon, Asmodeus, had posed as men throughout time, with a longstanding history of successful, sexual conquests of women, starting in Britannia shortly after the fall of the Roman Empire under the name of Cenric Moore, where he ravaged and killed forty-seven young maidens over a three year stretch before relocating to the Visigoth Kingdom, using a variety of bodies of handsome men for the slaughter and desecration of hundreds of women. Migrating to France in 856 and possessing the bodies of a French aristocrat named, Eustache Rennault and a Magistrate named, Jacques Puierout, he locked up sixty-six women in a closet of horrors, torturing and killing them one by one over a ninety-year period, carving up their bodies with a butcher knife like a gardener tending to soil and plants.

Weaving through Spain, Portugal, and the northern tip of Morocco from 1056 – 1375 AD, he killed thousands of women, working in earnest to hone his craft. It was during this time period that he began vaginal mutilation as a signature act of violation.

Working his way back north, he spent the next five centuries in Scotland, Wales, Ireland and rural parts of northern England, occupying the bodies of hundreds of handsome men ranging in age from twenty-seven to fifty-one. Carnage tallied over three thousand murdered and mutilated women. Before the world was so heavily populated, he could often safely kill without the aid of a human body, using his true features: a dark skinned, scaly creature with bat like wings, an elongated head with a mouth filled with serrated, needle-sharp teeth, long sharp talons at the end of long-thin arms, and legs that seemed to grow into the earth.

In 1847 he possessed the body of a handsome farmer in County Kerry, Ireland named Edward Flynn at the height of the horrific potato famine. It was easy to butcher hundreds of vulnerable, starving women in the rural parts of Southern Ireland amidst the blight of the famine, before moving north to Dublin and posturing as a police officer in charge of investigating the very crimes he was committing. *Oh, the irony of it stirs the libido!* The demon laughed.

Patrick James Ryan

Asmodeus leaned back from the railing, puffing on the tobacco, smiling and laughing at the utter incompetence and ignorance of the thousands of law-enforcement officials he duped over the course of the centuries in the never-ending quest to fulfill his insatiable lust for blood.

The American business man that Asmodeus sat next to at dinner walked around the corner of the starboard bow. The young man had blond hair and presented himself as a vibrant late twenty-something with the looks of a pampered aristocrat. Asmodeus decided it was time to discard the eighty-six-year-old body of Edward Flynn it had possessed and frozen in time for sixty-three years and move on to someone new. Approaching the young man, he smiled. "Barry Chadwick, if I recall from dinner?" the demon questioned with centuries of practiced charm.

"Why, yes. And you are the Irish investigator, Edward……"

"Flynn."

"Ah, yes. Lovely night."

"Yes indeed. I was wondering, Barry, if you could fill me in on some more of the enchanting engineering details of that moving vehicle called the Model T you are working on in America? It sounds like a wonderful investment opportunity." The demon smiled.

Chadwick blushed and smiled. "Most people aren't very interested. My wife is bored to tears by it"

"Well, I'm interested. Let's go grab a brandy and have a nice chat. With any luck, your wife will join us and I can regale her with blood curdling tales of my experience with crime."

"Well, as long as you don't scare her. She spooks easily," the naïve young man said.

"I assure you, I am very practiced in dealing with the fairer sex," Asmodeus smiled sarcastically, a nuance lost on the impressionable young man.

Patrick James Ryan

✝
Ma's Eats

The heifer shivered in spite of the heat, high humidity and claustrophobic living space. It had not been eating well the past few days, fear and adrenaline coursing through its body ever since witnessing one of its brethren carved up with a large knife three mornings ago. On that horrible day a man came into the adjacent cage and struck its male kin in the head with some type of metal object, and began slicing chunks of flesh from multiple parts of the body while the animal screamed and kicked until it was dead. The slicing and cutting went on with disturbing squishy sounds that made the heifer extremely uncomfortable and distraught.

In its diminished mind, it wondered when an attack like that was going to happen to it. It screamed on and off for hours until its throat hurt. Struggling, it shifted and squirmed in vain; tight steel shackles around a leg, allowing limited mobility around the cage and food trough. A nasty cut swelled through the skin and hair from the constant rubbing of the shackle. The beginning inklings of infection produced a pus-like discharge, a dirty shadow around the steel manacles that trapped the animal's leg.

Noises came from above and it paused from whimpering, ears perked, listening intently for signs of danger. It longed to be free again, out in the open to resume its former life, but the tight shackles promised a dark fate beyond comprehension.

***

It was a few seconds past 8:20 AM on a hot mid-July Saturday in the tiny town of Franklin, Arkansas, located in a very rural portion of the state. Franklin sat eighty miles south of the city of Arkadelphia and the dense Ouachita National Forest in the county of Hot Spring.

The sun was already pounding down on the gravel lot and adjacent swath of browned-out grass that served feebly for parking at the renowned, award-winning *Ma's Steak and Rib House*.

The long rectangular one-story wood-framed restaurant lay on a slab on the outskirts of town on Main Street about a quarter mile from the old, barren, weed-infested train station. The pine-wood structure was painted a dull, sun faded red, and sported an eight-by-eight-foot sign above the double door entrance, displaying a cartoon caricature of the lovable Ma Lubbock and a rotund cow sitting at a table full of meat. Both Ma and the cow were smiling, eagerly wearing bibs and holding silverware over sizzling steaks. The frontage of the building was humble, inviting and simple, exuding a homey gregariousness that made people smile and want to go inside.

Ma's Steak and Rib House was established with humble beginnings by Marian Lubbock and her husband Judd in the summer of 1988, when the Wilco Textile Factory folded and laid off half the town, including Judd Lubbock, who was trying to support a wife with two young sons and an infant daughter. "I

Patrick James Ryan

just knew they'd do dat to us…..shippin' all da jobs overseas…...bastards!" the thin, gray haired man must have said a thousand times after the layoffs.

Management always suppressed attempts to form a Union in lieu of profits, and the majority of workers never got past the eighth grade to have the capacity to even know how to challenge them, so the Lubbocks were hurting pretty badly financially after the layoff. Marian Lubbock saved the day by taking centuries-old family-cooking recipes and, along with her husband, turned them into one of the most popular eating establishments in all of Southern Arkansas.

Eventually the asbestos and factory chemical exposures sadly caught up with Judd, and Ma lost her beloved husband in 2006 to mesothelioma lung cancer. Her children, Judd, Jr; Lem, and Suzie, have helped with the popular eatery ever since.

Last night's patronage was a typical Friday evening at Ma's, a huge crowd, close to a ton of meat served, six kegs of beer drained, and several cases of Kentucky whiskey and bourbon consumed by the two thousand eight-hundred and forty guests over ten hours. Money was very good now, and the family did not want for material possessions or amenities beyond their humble lifestyle. Clientele was not always so abundant in the early days of the restaurant, and the Lubbocks struggled with overhead and quality food sources to stay within the budget, but once word of mouth spread and the reputation of Ma's fine cooking reached other areas of the state, people began driving from miles around just to dine on Ma's succulent recipes. The restaurant soon became a common weekend haven for students at the University of Arkansas in Little Rock to drive over to Ma's for a night of great steaks, ribs, sausage, pork chops, beer, pool and poker every Friday. It was certainly not an exaggeration to say *Ma's Steak and Rib House* was now a veritable hangout with regulars, who came in two to three times a week, and repeat customers at least every month.

Cashed rolled in and Ma now proudly owns a seven-acre farm where grass-fed bulls and cows graze in open green fields, and a barn full of chickens and pigs fatten themselves up for their ultimate destination on tables at *Ma's Steak and Rib House*.

Like most Friday nights, more than a handful of patrons were too drunk to drive, and sometimes cars piled up from week to week unclaimed. Ma established a rule that any car unclaimed after a month would go to Bennie's Automotive Service Shop over on Maple Street for sale at the auction on the fifteenth of each month. Ma split the money with Bennie and held it in an escrow account down at the bank for six months just in case a sheepish owner, or angry parent showed up to claim the abandoned property. Bennie swore that some people left the cars on purpose, reporting them stolen to get the insurance money. Ma initially rebuffed that notion, having more faith in people, but the new generation seemed to lack moral substance in many instances. "All dem damn kidz do iz mess wit dat dumb textin' on dem damn cell phones!" Ma would say at least once a week, rolling her eyes while her kids laughed.

Judd, Jr. and Lem dreaded Saturday mornings because so much work needed to be done getting the restaurant cleaned up from Friday night's crowd before the cycle started all over again, until they took Sunday afternoon and evening off in homage to the

Lord, right after Ma's famous All You Can Eat Sunday breakfast buffet from 7:00 to noon. Mayor Pursell had an indefinite standing reservation on Sunday for three eggs, sausage, bacon and grits with gravy

"Hey, Lem, Ma says to take dem cars oe'r to Bennie's for ser-va-sin. She said she done tolt ya now three times, ya lazy fuck!"

"Ah, fuck you, Judd! I'm tired of doin' da cars all da time!" the younger brother said, challenging his older, much stronger sibling.

Judd frowned; rugged cheeks flushed with anger at the impertinence from his little brother. "Ya noze da deal, lil' Brutha. I does da kitchen and cure da meat, Ma duz da cookin', Suzy serves da customers and you duz all da grunt stuff, like da cars!"

The younger boy put his head down dejected. He knew he was the grunt in the family, last on the totem pole for all the dirty jobs no one else wanted to do. *Lem, wash out da pig barn stalls. Lem, take da cars to Bernie's. Lem, clean up da vomit in da Men's Room from da rembunkshuss college kid who puked in da sink. Lem, plunge da toilet from da girl, who took a massive shit an' clogged it with too much toilet paper. Lem, get da trash.* He resented the subordinate role and continued to press the issue with his brother. "Y'all git ta do da important stuff and I git all da shit!"

Judd sneered, growing tired of his brother's incessant whining. "Ain't my fault I came outta Ma's belly ba-fore ya! Basides, County Fair's cummin' up next month, and Ma's nervas as shit 'bout it! She don't want to looz first place at da Rib Fest. Ya know she done won it da past seventeen years runnin', but all dem others are cummin' in now with dat big-city money just ta compete wit Ma! She's already shittin' herself oe'r it! Don't go makin' trubble for her....and ya knows dat scout from dat Food Network show we saw last year keeps callin' and is sposed' to come again next month, and she's worried 'bout it!"

"What's da Fair and Ma talkin' to da Food Network guy got ta do wit me and doin all da grunt shit?"

The older boy, age twenty-nine, smacked his twenty-six-year old little brother on the back of the head with his palm; a playful mentoring tap. "Ma don't want nobuddy makin' waves or changin' da routine dis close to da Fair!"

"Well, I'ze sick of cleanin' up all da shit from da bulls in the slaughterhouse at da farm, and those little heifers make messes in der cages, too, downstairs! Why can't we hire sumbuddy ta do it and I can help in da restraunt?"

The older boy shook his head, clearly getting frustrated over his little brother's relentless complaining. "Dammit, Lem, weeze a famly bizness and Ma don't want no outsiders. Basides, what if someone outside da famly done stole some of Ma's recipes and solt dem to some big corprashun?"

Lem shrugged.

"Uh huh." Judd nodded his head. "Dat's right. We'd be fucked like a cyote in a bear trap! Basides, you talk too damn much when ya drink whiskey. Dat's why Ma don't want ya doin' da meat in da restraunt. What if ya let sumthin' slip bout her secret recipes?"

The younger brother frowned again, not giving up on the argument. "Wat if sumthin' happened to ya, Judd? Whooze goona do da meat then?"

The older boy opened his mouth to speak and paused. The question had never been posed before, and other than when they lost their father, the notion of their own mortality was almost incomprehensible to the boys.

Sensing some traction in the discussion, Lem continued. "I mean, you kin awways do da cars and other shit if sumthin' happened to me, but I ain't no good at all at da meat and cookin's stuff. Who'd help Ma? She's gittin' older. Ain't it 'bout time I git some trainin' on da meat?"

Judd frowned, pursing his lips while a tiny furrow formed in the skin below his brow. His younger brother held his breath, watching Judd think and digest the infallible point. It was a valid, persuasive argument. After a minute, which seemed like ten to Lem, Judd began to nod his head.

"Okay, Lem. Follow me."

Lem lit up like a five-year old coming down the steps on Christmas morning. "Really?"

"Yep. Ya make a good point, lil Brutha. Don't tell Ma just yet dat Ize teachin' ya. We'll tell her later. Okay?"

Lem smiled and nodded his head, still expressing childlike exuberance and enthusiasm.

"Good. She's been meaner than a rattler oe'r this Food Network shit and the upcoming fair."

"Ya, I noticed," Lem said.

Judd led his little brother behind the restaurant along the gravel lot to the rear of the property, facing a densely wooded area with a stream in the distance, and approached a sixteen-by-thirty-foot cement patio that abutted the rear of the restaurant. Judd stuck his nose up, frowning. A large dumpster was stuffed with crates of barbeque sauce jars, pasta noodle boxes, potato boxes, scores of bottles of salad dressings used for marinades, hundreds of liquor bottles, and a slew of paper products. Flies cluttered the vicinity like confetti on New Year's Eve.

"Damn trash stinks! Pisses me off dey only come ta empty it evry otha week, instead of weekly like they'ze spose ta do! It's ok for dem ta be late, but they'd be shittin' bricks, if we was late on da propty taxes!"

Judd unlocked a heavily padlocked, steel double door, allowing access to twelve concrete steps that led down to a massive basement underneath the restaurant. Judd led the way, pausing on step five, and turned to his brother.

"Dare's ten rooms wit livestock, two large, walk-in coolers fer frozin' meat storage, da meat carvin' room, and da room where I git rid of all da waste and shit dat Ma don't use." Lem nodded with growing excitement and eager anticipation.

"We'll start wit da meat coolers and I'll show ya da diffrant cuts of meat and how Ma serves em. Then ya best git dem cars before she start screamin' murder. Afta lunch I'll show ya how ta carve da meat. I'm thawin' out some flank from a bull and the torsos of a couple little heifers.

"I like da little heifers," Lem grinned. "Dare tasty! Yum, yum!"

"Dare won't be no time fer fuckin' round, Lem. Specially on a Satraday. We could be slammed agin jus like last night."

Lem nodded, his demeanor changing to serious as quickly as a faucet being turned off. He did not want to fuck up this rare opportunity to impress his older brother.

"Awright, when we git to da bottom, turn left and I'll take ya to meat locker number one."

A few minutes later Lem shivered in the frigid locker, staring in fascination and listening to Judd define the various locations and cuts of meat and how they factored into the entrees offered by Ma. Eight sections of five-foot chunks of meat were impaled mid-way up on large steel hooks with a white, opaque sheet of ice covering the red tissue, white bone and yellow, subcutaneous fat. Five out of the eight sported boisterous girth that Judd identified as full-grown cows. The other three were much thinner, muscular heifers and little bulls that Judd explained Ma used for veal, a ground chili mix, baby back ribs, steak sandwiches and several brisket recipes.

Judd continued. "Dis meat will be used the next five weeks. Dare's two sections in da butcher room in da back. One iz where I carve off skin and fat from da animals to git to da edabull meat. Then I freeze it in da two meat lockers until I need ta cut it up ta be ready fer da kitchen. Dat's when I thaw it out in da butcher-block room fer carvin' inta servin' size.

Lem nodded intently, the thirsty apprentice, eager to learn the craft of the business.

"Ok, dat's enuff fer today. Ya best git dem cars now and feed da hogs and cows in da barn, and spray out da cages. I'll feed da little heifers and bulls in here."

***

Lem drove back from Bennie's Service Center after the third and final trip in the tow truck to drop off a Ford Escape. It must have been Ford week, he thought, as the previous two vehicles towed were a Taurus and a beautiful, brand new Edge.

It had taken him an hour and forty-five minutes to do the cars, and an hour and a half to water down the animal cages at the farm, spray the pigs off, settle down four of the cows, who were still very disheveled and upset from the recent move from the open field to the barn cages - almost as if they could sense their days were numbered - and load the food troughs. He was exhausted, sweaty and hungry; surviving on adrenaline and the anticipation of learning more about the nuances of the family business from Judd. He was in no mood to deal with a pushy city-slicker.

When Lem turned off Main Street and cruised down the half mile to Ma's Eat's at the intersection of Main and Station Drive, he saw a colorful van sitting in the gravel lot with a name on the side that read: 'Hillbilly Cookin."

Two men stood by the van talking to Judd wearing khakis and blue and black polo shirts. One was short and stocky with a significant receding hairline of black locks that lamely covered a horrible comb-over. Comb-over man was holding a camera, fidgeting, while his partner stood just to the right next to Judd. The taller, thinner man had brown hair and talked incessantly, gesturing like an old snake oil salesman, while Judd sighed, rolled his eyes, and shook his head.

"Wat in da hell iz dis shit?" Lem muttered to himself, parking the tow truck off to the side in the grass. Approaching the conversation from the rear, Lem heard Judd's exasperation.

"I done tolt ya she's doin' da books and ain't got no time taday to talk wit ya!"

The pushy man stood several inches over Judd and looked down at him in frustration, raising his hands and spinning around like a peacock flapping its wings. "Judd, I'm sure that if your mother just knew who we are and how interested we are in hiring her to do a TV show on the Food Network, she'd talk to us!"

"I remember youze guys. Y'all been here before."

"Wat's goin on?" Lem asked.

Both men jumped, startled, whirling around to face Lem. The tall talkative man looked Lem up and down for several seconds as if scrutinizing a new breed of insect before seizing the moment to win over another family member, who could be manipulated.

"You must be the little brother, Lem?"

Lem stiffened at the open acknowledgement of being little brother. "Wat duh ya want, mister?"

The brown-haired man's upper lip curled up on the right side; a subtle hint of disingenuousness that Lem subconsciously honed in on, creating instant distrust. "My name is Marvin Camden from the Food Network TV Show, Hillbilly Cooking." Marvin held his hand out to shake with Lem and was met with a blank stare. Slightly ruffled, he retracted his hand and continued. "You see, we've heard about how awesome your mom's food is and thought she would make a perfect fit on our new show." Smiling, he waited five painful seconds for Lem to respond. Lem continued the blank stare before finally speaking.

"Ain't ya sposed ta be here two weeks from now?"

The man shifted his feet nervously, nodding his head. "Yes. Yes. But, we drove for eighteen hours and thought we could at least meet with your mom again and discuss our offer."

Ya lyin' fleck of maggot shit. Ya just want to use Ma to make money off of her! Lem thought but kept his cool, just like Ma taught him. You could never trust an outsider, Ma always taught them.

"Like Judd said, Ma's doin' paypa work right now."

The man frowned. "Can't you boys at least let her know we are here and will be in the area through Sunday?"

Judd stepped up between the man and his brother. "Look mista, we don't like pushy folk like ya, so quit buggin' us. I'll go tell Ma you all iz here."

The man smiled and walked back over to his colleague, instantly disregarding Lem like he was not there and began to whisper to the shorter, chubbier man. Judd came back out five minutes later. "Ma said to come over on Sunday afternoon at 2:00, and ya only got a half hour cause dat's her only time off."

Marvin Camden smiled and said, "We will see you then, boys, and tell your mom thanks!"

***

The short, chubby-cheeked, heavy set woman with overly dyed auburn hair shifted on the bar stool. She was wearing clown like make up, lavender eye shadow to excess, caked rouge and an out-of-style purple pant suit. She took the palm of her left hand

and placed it at the base of the mid-fifties bee hive haircut like Atlas holding up the world. A witty observer could have parodied in earnest that Jimmy Hoffa's body could reasonably be hidden in the mountainous bee hive hairdoo.

Marian Lubbock finished checking the base of the hair and rolled her eyes, adjusting the bar stool she sat on and looking at Judd, Lem and Suzy across the table.

"Well, shit! I don't need dis city fuck cummin' in ta watch us and bother us from servin' custamers! We gotz us a ruteen and I don't like change!"

Suzy, sitting pretty like a fresh-faced porn star, taking after her father's striking good looks, nodded her head in agreement, mired in perpetual placation of her mother. She was Charlie McCarthy to Ma's Edgar Bergen.

"Well, don't jus sit dere like lumps. Wat do ya think, Boys?" Ma asked wanting Judd's ultimate opinion, but including Lem so he would not feel slighted.

Judd shrugged. "Da man dit say it would be a lot of money."

Ma put her hands up in a warding off gesture, shaking her head, chubby jowls shaking back and forth like jello. "No...no....no...we don't need no more money. Ba-sides, all the fussin' and tenshun' will jus bring in more outsiders, who would botha da reglar custamers. No, I'm gainst' it!"

Judd shook his head while Lem looked back and forth between brother and mother like watching a tennis match. "Well, he's cummin' Sunday afternoon, Ma. Ya said yerself it was ok. Jus let im say his pitch and tell im no thanks," Judd said.

Ma rolled her eyes, false eyelashes fluttering like a hummingbird, and slid off the bar stool, signifying the end of the conversation. "Awright, Judd. I'll listen to im Sunday, but we ain't doin' it. Let's jus git it oer' with. C'mon, Evrabuddy, we gots to git ready fer tonight!"

The family moved quickly, knowing time was short before the Happy Hour crowd started filtering in.

***

The butcher room underneath the restaurant was sweltering and the fan in the corner did little to quell the perspiration that poured off the bodies of the two brothers. Lem watched Judd maneuver and prepare to cut chunks of meat and tissue from a thawed out little heifer on the butcher's counter in spellbound fascination. Lem crossed his legs back and forth to deter any embarrassment from the growing erection in his pants.

Enamored with the task at hand, Judd would have never noticed his little brother's arousal. "Okay, fore I start, let me back track a bit. I already cut off the head and let the blood drain so it ain't so messy wit what we doin' now. I sawed inta da skull to get da brains. Wit da little animals, Ma likes ta put dem in her beef and noodles recipe." Judd smiled. "Tender as shit, and customers love it!"

Lem nodded, a bit of drool collecting at the corner of his mouth like Pavlov's dog at the mention of the beef and noodles.

"Then I git out da buck skinning knife and carve off da skin. Dis takes fuckin' forever sometimes, specially wit da big cows and bulls. Da pigs is pretty easy though. Then I gut it wit da big cleaver to git rid of all da shit and innards up inside the belly and testines. It's easy with these little calfs. I can hang dem on the big hook and do it, but da cows and big bulls iz a bitch! I got's ta do dem on da floor. Then I cut the limbs off wit da saw. Sum of da meat on the limbs Ma uses, but da bulk of da cuts comes from da torso, back, flank and loin. Once I'ze done guttin' it, I start on the quawlty cuts. Got dat so far, Little Brutha?"

Lem nodded again, excitement building. "How long does it take ya to do all dat fore ya git ta dis point?"

Judd pursed his lips back and forth, pondering the question. "The cows take all day long and I usually do em on Wensdays. I can sometimes do dese little heifers and calfs in three hours."

"Wow! Dat's allota work!" Lem whistled.

"Damn right! Okay. Let me teach ya da cuts now."

Judd lined up a cleaver, hacksaw, several long blades and a hatchet. He positioned the animal's torso and took the cleaver and a long cutting knife, carving deep incisions into the stomach.

"Da belly's good for flank steak and briskets. Da ribs is used for roasts, rib eye steaks, and barbeque with Ma's special sauce. Ma uses the loin for veal parmigiana and filet mignon. On the big cows she uses da shoulder for most of da steaks. It's good chuck meat. Da sirloin cuts come from da lower back and top of the round."

Forty-five minutes later the carcass was professionally divided up and a drenched, exhausted

Judd paused and smiled. "It's harder than ya thought, eh, Lil Brutha?"

Lem smiled. "I think I best watch ya a while fore I try doin' it myself."

Judd set down the bloody cleaver and hugged his little brother. "Dat's how Dad taught me, and I'll teach ya. I'll show ya some more Sunday morning.' Now, help me put dese cuts in plastic wrap and take 'em on up to da kitchen fridge."

***

Cigarette smoke filled the restaurant and several hundred patrons packed *Ma's Steak and Rib House* wall to wall by 7:00 PM Saturday night, testing the limits of the buildings air conditioner and patience of the employees. Two distinct cultures vied for attention in separate sections of the restaurant. The usual crowd of students from Little Rock dominated the pool table and sports bar area, drinking generous quantities of beer, pounding down shots of Kentucky whiskey, ordering ribs, nachos, chili and burgers, and pushing the decibel limit on noise, while the quieter, unpretentious town regulars preferred the booth section to engage in casual conversation and dine on Ma's succulent steaks with the popular loaded cheesy baked potato side accompanied with the best onion rings in the state, or Ma's famous three-cheese blend of Mac N' Cheese.

A combination of two subsets of customers stood around in the foyer and bar with an average wait of an hour for a booth or table. With patrons busting the seams on Fridays and Saturdays, Ma typically brought in extra part-time employees to handle the overflow.

Patrick James Ryan

Jimmy Harper joined Chris Jones behind the bar, and Valerie Meek, Ronda Phillips, Julia Prescott, and Hilary Skinner joined Suzy, Patti Stewart, and Rachel Chandler serving tables, while Lem and his best friend, Skipper Gillette, son of town sheriff, Arthur Gillette, bussed tables.

Ma personally supervised the cooking by hand picking cuts of meat and mentoring long-term chef protégés, Billy Chester and Harmony Jones, wife of bartender Chris Jones. Once per hour Ma would circulate throughout the restaurant, greeting patrons, checking on meals and service, and gathering cash from the bar registers to put back in the safe in the kitchen. She rotated pink, black and lavender tent sized dresses framing her copious girth like old hotel drapes to compliment generous pounds of facial make up.

At half past ten, Ma was making rounds through the restaurant and observed four girls and two boys from the sports bar area glaringly intoxicated. She tapped Suzy on the shoulder on the way back to the kitchen, a signal Suzy knew meant to meet in the kitchen to talk in private.

"Whatcha need, Ma?" the voluptuous blonde said, sashaying into the kitchen, catching the eye of chef, Billy Chester, one of the few things in the world that could distract the master cook from his craft.

Ma frowned, jowls forming a third chin like a chubby man's ass cheeks pressed against the side of someone's' face. "Got some drunks in da bar area already! Didja see Mayor Carmichael's gotz family in from Miss-sipi?"

Suzy shook her head.

"Well, they'ze all in dat corner, round booth, all eight of 'em, and dey can see right in da bar from dere! Best git Judd, Lem, Skipper and Chris Jones on it right away!"

Suzy looked at the clock above the grill. "Okay Ma, but ain't it a bit early to start clearin' out some of da young-uns? Won't it cause more utenshun dis early?"

Ma Lubbock scoffed at her daughter, raising eyebrows that were almost completely eclipsed by the jet-black false eyelashes. "They'ze drunk, Suzy! I want 'em outta here now, not later. The sooner them boyz get at it, da less hassle later. Ya got me, Girl?"

Suzy lifted thickly red lip-sticked lips in a slight pout, a facial expression purveyors of porn would coach endlessly to star wannabes for hours to master, but came naturally to Suzy. She nodded and left the kitchen.

Judd frowned when his little sister relayed Ma's orders. "Shit! Awright. Lemme tell Chris. You go tell Lem ta unlock the back cellar door and git Skipper. We'll put 'em down dere til dey sober up or the crowd thins out."

Suzy smiled and rubbed her chest against Judd's muscular right arm. "Be careful. Big Brutha."

Judd smiled back. "Yew is such a lil flirt, Girl! Now git and go tell Lem and Skipper…..hey, make sure dey bring da plastic in case one of 'em pukes!"

Suzy nodded and dropped the seductive veneer.

***

At 3:10 AM, Chris Jones declared last call at the bar and shortly thereafter regulars, Rusty Pinkerton and Griff Henson, finished off their seventeenth and thirteenth beers respectively, stumbling out the door to walk the mile and a half back to their flats on Robert E. Lee Boulevard.

A hazy fog clogged the air, as Judd locked the front door and the remaining employees comprised of Chris and Harmony Jones, Judd, Lem, Skipper, Suzy and Ma congregated around a high table in the sports section near the bar.

"Whew, what a night!" Chris Jones said. "Me and Harmony gonna hit da road. Gugh-night ya'all!"

Skipper said to Judd and Lem after the Jones' left. "How many drunks ya got below?"

Judd shrugged and knew why Skipper was asking the question. "Lost count....ten....maybe twelve. A cupple of 'em ain't got no ID. Have yer dad come oe'r round 11:00. I'll be up and we can git da ones dat sober anuff oe'r to da station. We'll tend to da others once dey come to."

The tall, rail-thin boy with carrot-colored hair and heavy facial freckles gave Judd a thumbs-up. "Will do. See y'all."

Judd, Lem and Suzy turned to Ma, who looked exhausted and about to collapse but still lucid enough to bark out orders. "Okay kids. Anutha good night. I think da bar made a record on sales. We got lots a work tamarra and some of doze yung-uns to tend to, so let's hit da hay."

Judd tapped his mother on the shoulder. "Don't forgit dat man from da Food Network's coming at 2:00 tamarra."

Ma flinched and then stomped her left foot down on the floor. "AW SHIT.........! cancel it!"

"Ma, I can't cancel it. He didn't give me no card or number. No way to call 'em!" Judd said.

"AH, WELL STUFF A GOPHER UP MY ASS! FUCK!" she hollered and pouted, sitting back down on the bar stool. A few seconds later, she bounced back up. "Awright. We'll see wat he has ta say! If I still feel the way I do now 'bout it, then I noze what I'z gonna tell im!"

The kids smiled at each other, chuckling under their breath.

***

Ma Lubbock squinted uncomfortably in the glare from the tall lights set up on tripods situated in a triangle by Marvin Camden's camera man from the Food Network show, Hillbilly Cooking. The heat from the lights was making Ma sweat through the lavender colored dress, and the curls of her dyed auburn hair were matted and sticky, making her feel tense and irritated. The tight-wicker chair they brought for a prop dug into the folds of fat around her hips and waist, making her feel self-conscious of her generous girth. Suzy, Lem, and Judd stood behind the tripods in a supportive role while Marvin Camden flitted about with the cameraman in preparation for the interview.

Camden sat down adjacent to Ma in one of the two large brown wicker chairs brought in for the interview. The camera man panned over to Camden, smiling, polished and already in show-time mode.

"Hi there, Folks! This is Marvin Camden from Hillbilly Cookin'! How ya'all doin?" Camden said with fake southern country emphasis that made all of the

Patrick James Ryan

Lubbocks cringe. "We're here at the famous Ma's Steak and Rib House in Franklin, Arkansas where the locals swear the steaks, ribs, chili and burgers are the best in the world, and where people come to dine from all over the South!"

Lyin' piece of shit! Ma thought, disdain and distrust fueling her preconceived notion of TV people. *We don't git people from all o'er da South, ya phony shit-licker!*

Camden continued. "We have none other than the owner and proprietor of Ma's Steak and Rib House, Marian Lubbock…..Ms. Lubbock, thanks for having us in from Hillbilly Cookin' today!"

Ma swallowed, allowing herself a second for composure and dissipation of anger and uttered the phrase she had said thousands of times greeting customers over the years, "Welcome ta Ma's Steak and Rib House. We're all darn happy to ave ya!"

"Thank you Ms. Lubbock. Great to be here!"

Stepping into character, she smiled. "Ya kin call me Ma, Marvin."

"Thanks, Ma!" the cheesy TV man said. "Before you cook us up something from that famous kitchen of yours, let me ask you a question everyone is dying to know…..what is your favorite dish?"

Ma was pleasantly surprised and taken off guard slightly. Smiling, she blushed and began gesturing with her hands like a Sunday Preacher. "Well, I love em all, but da one I'ze been most proud of iz da Filet Osca with Veal Giblets and my special béarnaise sauce. It's a com-nation of things my Ma and Pa done taught me when I'ze a lil girl, and the people love it!"

Camden smiled with practiced indifference that conveyed fake empathy and interest, and concealed boredom and impatience, an expression not completely lost on Ma, who was a master at reading people.

"Well, that's just marvelous, Ma," Camden said, barely disguising his placating tone. He paused and pursed his lips, feigning thought and care. "Let me ask you a question about something that is a little controversial and may potentially turn off some viewers, when we have you on the show."

Ma shifted in the wicker chair like a hippo stuck in the mud, clearly beginning to get agitated from Camden's preface to a question she anticipated was going to piss her off.

"Several of your dishes contain veal, including the family favorite you just mentioned. Everyone at the Network, including me, loved the restaurant when we first visited last year, but as a national TV show, we have to vet out any possible controversy that would bring undo scrutiny or negative attention."

Ma looked puzzled. *They'ze gonna bring a Corvette on da show here?* Frowning, Ma gave Camden a stern stare. "Young man, ya jus lost me wit all doze big words! What the Sam Hill iz ya talkin' bout?"

Camden reddened with embarrassment. "I'm sorry, Ma. What I'm trying to say is some people think the way veal is made is inhumane and cruel to the calves. You know, starving them, putting them in cages for months, all the things you read."

Ma rolled her eyes and waved her hand, as if it had power to ward off such a ridiculous notion about veal. "Well, let me tell ya, all our animals iz well fed. Some of da little heifers we chooze for veal iz kept in a cage, but fer no more dan a week, and well cared fer. Theeze assholes don't know wat would happen if too many animals popalated the cuntreeside. Pardon my words, Mr. Camden." She smiled at the big TV producer with a charm that lulled many into her spider web of control over the years.

Camden smiled. "No, I understand and I agree."

Ma grinned in appreciation and looked deep into Camden's eyes, finalizing a decision she'd been debating and asked the question that triggered a plan. "Would ya like ta see how we does it?"

Wondering how he lost control of the interview, Camden stuttered. "I...I still need to....to finish my questions, Ma....I have to….."

"Let's take a break." Ma said, now completely in charge. "My bottom feels like dis chair jus took a bite out of it! I shows ya da kitchen now and Lem and Judd can take your camera boy down where we cut the meat up soze ya don't think wee'ze torcherin da animals! Okay?"

Camden paused and looked over at the cameraman, who shrugged and twerked his shoulder, putting the camera down, resigning himself to the inevitable break.

"Okay, I guess we can take a tour, Ma. My cameraman is Jeff Phillips."

Ma smiled again. "Da boyz can take Jeff down to the storage and meat cutting rooms and Suzy and me will show ya da kitchen."

Camden nodded and the two groups broke up, going their separate ways.

***

"And dat's how we mange da flow between da three fridgerators and the grill for Billy and Harmony. Da salad bar can be used by da customers and we add fresh greens and veggies evry two hours...." Ma paused and took a deep breath. "Well, dats bout it."

Camden felt exhausted. Ma had been talking non-stop for the last forty minutes and he was having some doubts about her effectiveness on TV if she talked so incessantly. However, the operation and quality of the food was impressive. She was definitely going to need some coaching and polishing for television, and definitely some new clothes and make up. He was extremely impressed with the organization and flow of the business. For not having any formal education, Ma could teach a lot of the so-called dime-a-dozen MBA's about how to actually run a business. She had quickly heated up a bowl of her chili, a left over from the night before. It was simply divine and Camden continued to rave about it. "Ma, I think that was the best chili I've ever had! What all is in that?"

Ma smiled and blushed. "It's a mix of flavored sausage from da pigs, a few chunks of Veal, and ground sirloin. I done uze a com-nation of pinto and kinney beans for da flavor, and my sauce is a secret."

Suzy smiled and winked at her mother. Camden immediately noticed the exchange and laughed. "Ok, I get it. Secret family recipe?"

Suzy laughed out loud seductively. "I guess ya could say dat, Mr. Camden."

Camden stared at the attractive girl, soaking in her sexuality and feeling the narcotic effect of her persona and body. Shaking himself slightly, he glanced at his watch. "Hey, we better go get Jeff and wrap up the interview back out in the restaurant."

Ma smiled. "Sure. We'll take ya down ourselves.

***

Patrick James Ryan

The steps and walls that led from the kitchen to the basement beneath the restaurant were a dull, drab, cement gray. Cob webs adorned corners, crevices and the ceiling. A cool draft rose from the meat lockers, instantly dropping the temperature in the stairwell a good fifteen degrees. Camden shivered, wedged between Suzy in the lead and Ma to his rear, going down the steps.

"Kind of chilly here on the steps, huh?"

Suzy turned around and smirked, ignoring the question. "We'll turn left at da bottom."

They reached the floor and Ma took over, holding a skeleton key chain harboring about a dozen keys. "In dis first door we got frozin' slabs of beef from da cows." She unlocked the door and Camden peered in through large double steel doors, seeing several rows of five-foot slabs of beef hanging on large metal hooks. The reddish pink tissue displayed very little fat and looked rich and vibrant.

"Like I tolt ya, they'ze all grass fed cows with jusanuff fat fer da best flavor around."

Camden smiled, growing more impressed with the operation by the minute.

Ma and Suzy led him past two more large metal doors. "Deeze iz more coolers. One is fer da pigs and lil heifers we carve and freeze fer some of da specialtee dishes. The otha is fer more cow meat."

Camden nodded, again impressed by the size and magnitude of the little family- owned restaurant. Looking at a large, double steel door at the end of the hallway, he noticed traces of blood on the floor and a streak on the glistening metal door. The temperature rose significantly and he could start to see beads of condensation, sweating on the outside of the steel metal doors. "What is that room at the end for?"

Ma stared hard at the man, and Suzy stopped in her tracks and turned, making eye contact with Camden with an absence of the former lecherous nature; replaced by a cold ambivalent stare. Five ugly seconds passed and Camden felt sweat trickle down the back of his neck, stomach suddenly gurgling.

Ma finally broke the awkward silence. "Well, Mr. Camden, dats where we carve up da meat. I don't know if you'ze wants to see dat, though. It's pretty yucky in dere!"

Camden smiled sheepishly and looked down at his feet. "That's ok. I just saw the blood and I guess it spooked me a little.

Suzy cast a quick glimpse at her mother and smirked. Ma smiled with genuine empathy. "Dat's okay, Mr. Camden. Da meat bidness can be a bloody bidness sometimes."

Camden nodded, regaining some of the composure and confidence, suddenly realizing it had been over an hour since they took a break from the interview. "I understand. Hey, where's Jeff and your sons?"

Ma looked at Suzy with a perplexed expression and Suzy shrugged. "I don't rightly know. We shoulda passed 'em unless da boyz took im out in the back lot."

Camden looked up and down the empty corridor, inklings of discomfort beginning to return. "It's been a while and we really ought to all go back upstairs and continue the interview."

"I guess we could check da butcher room, but I don't know why they'd go in dere?" Ma said.

Camden shrugged. "Sure. Why not? At the very least, I'm getting a hands-on education of the industry," he said, smiling again.

Ma nodded her head and Suzy winked at Camden, marking the return of the flirtatious demeanor. They walked down the corridor to the ominous, perspiring metal doors, looming sentinels to a house of slaughter, and Camden's heart began to beat rapidly. The temperature seemed to rise with each step and the soupy humidity was palpable.

They reached the doors and Ma fumbled momentarily, searching for one of the keys on the keychain. Turning, she smiled. "Now itz pretty messy in dere, Mr. Camden. Ya sure ya'all still want to go in?"

Marvin Camden smiled with a soothing facial expression. "Don't worry about me, Ma. I am sure I can handle a little blood and guts."

Ma winked at him and opened the left panel door. "After ya, Marvin."

Camden eased his way into the room. On first inspection, the room was brightly lit, almost blindingly so after spending several minutes in the dim, sterile hallway outside. Bright white walls connected to a white tile floor. Several cages were spaced apart along the walls containing little heifers. A huge stainless-steel sink was flanked by a large wood butcher's block. Camden's eyes slowly adjusted to the light. Judd was busy carving up a huge chunk of meat on the block. A baby calf was in the first cage to his left along the wall, skinny, frail and sad. It mooed at Camden and he knew it was a cry for help.

Camden looked at the next cage and gasped. A naked, young blonde-haired girl was shackled to the wall. Her hair was matted to her skull from the terrible humidity in the room. Several nasty cuts and bruises were visible on her face, chest stomach and legs; angry vestiges of incomprehensible abuse. She saw Camden and struggled against the steel shackle cutting into her ankle, agitating the yellowish, pus-filled infection that assaulted the skin and tissue around the bone.

"Help me. Please help me!" she squeaked out.

Camden's mouth dropped and he continued to stare. Another naked young girl, browned haired and well built, was unconscious in a cage next to the blonde, equally defiled, dirty and bloodied. A naked young man was in a cage on the wall perpendicular to the girls. His chest had been sliced open from neck to groin. The rib cage lay open, cut down the center. The right side of the rib cage was missing, along with all the internal organs from the torso, eviscerated and cut out for a variety of Ma's secret recipes. Camden fought back the Chili, now rising up in his throat until a wet, slicing noise made him look over toward the butcher's table.

Cameraman, Jeff Phillips was spread out on the big board, naked on his stomach; head tilted over the edge as Judd sliced a huge, very deep gash across his throat with a gigantic, razor sharp knife, and let the head plop down over the edge of the table. Blood poured out from the severed arteries into a large bucket. Judd smiled. "We'll need to git this thick, rich blood inta the fridge right away, if wee'ze gonna use it for sauce. Ba-sides, when I done saw inta his brain fer da veal cutlets, I wants all the blood drained so I got less mess." He winked at Camden.

The master wordsmith and vocal charmer was at a complete loss for words. Terror stricken, he could not move his arms and legs, and struggled for speech. "Wha....what....why? Why are you....?"

Judd winked at him. "Ya see all dat chubby flesh on his ass? Dat will be purrfect fer sausage and bacon fer next week's Sunday brunch. Them chunky thighs will make for a filet or two, and I jus love da liver and onions Ma makes!"

Camden slowly moved his body around to face Suzy and Ma, face ashen and pale; sweat pouring off his body. "Please....I must go now...I won't tell anyone......you don't need to be on the show. Please, I have to....."

Ma stared a hole through Camden's face. "Yoo ain't goin' nowhere, fucker!" she said in a menacing tone that scared Camden almost as much as the macabre debauchery visualized throughout the room. Gone was the hillbilly, matronly façade put on for the interview upstairs. Looking into her eyes, he knew as sure as looking down the barrel of a gun, that she was a stone cold, insane killer.

He spun back around and Lem was suddenly right in front of him. *Where the hell did he come from?* Camden thought, bewildered. Lem's right hand swung up in an arc toward Camden's face, striking him across the left side of the head and chin with a small billy club. Camden went down like a boxer who was just TKO'd.

Ma smiled and nodded. "Awright! Let's clean up dis mess. Lots of work, kids! Lem, wee'ze got cars to git to Bennie's from last night and I wants all dat camera crap stuff burnt. Take dat silly van and drive it into da river."

Lem rolled his eyes. "Ah Ma, can't I do dat stuff later?"

"No! First dings first. Do it now and den ya can let Judd teach ya some more down here."

Lem recoiled and turned on Judd. "Ya tolt her? I thought ya said to keep it tween us?"

Judd shook his head. "I didn't tell."

Ma smiled at her sons. "Yoo boyz still think I don't noze stuff. I noze evrathing dat goes on round here!"

Suzy laughed and crossed her index fingers back and forth, signifying the boys had been bad.

Ma laughed. "It's okay, boyz! I think it is time for Lem to learn more 'bout the family bidness. We gonna have lots to carve up dis week!"

Patrick James Ryan

Author's Notes

Well, I hope you enjoyed this collection of short stories. This is my second collection of stories following ***Blood Verse,*** which was published in 2013 and recently re-released with updates, edits and expansions of some of the stories, also through ***Black Bed Sheet Books***.

On the heel of the success of ***Blood Verse,*** I was frequently asked by interviewers and people at book-signings how I get my ideas. At times it made for great discussion, but is also made me lament that readers were getting cheated out of some context and clarity behind the stories in ***Blood Verse***. Likewise, I've read some terrific work from a variety of authors over the years, and many a time wondered what prompted them to tell the tale? What was the trigger or inspiration for that story? How did they come up with the idea for the story about this and that…and on and on. When ***Blood Verse*** was re-released in 2016, I added some author notes with reservations, but received excellent reader feedback.

At the risk of being self-indulgent again, and bending the writer's cardinal rule that a good story should sell itself without any additional explanation, I am taking a few liberties here to add some insight behind this collection of stories. Have fun exploring my warped mind.

Over The Edge:

Ok, everyone loves a good werewolf tale, and I hope you would call this one a good tale. There is something very feral, carnal, interesting and titillating about the notion of a human transforming into a monstrous, powerful beast. I've read dozens and dozens of werewolf stories from Stephen King's classic, *Cycle of the Werewolf,* to Gary Brandner's innovative, *The Howling,* to Robert R. McCammon's *Wolf's Hour,* to countless werewolf anthologies by great authors. This is my humble attempt to dive into Werewolf noir with a slightly different twist. In *Over the Edge*, I chose to establish stress and anxiety as triggers for Lycanthropy. Not a full moon, although that may have been implied to enable readers to make up their own minds? Also the origin is not necessarily a bite from a wolf, but it could have been. Let readers add their own origin in addition to the stress angle! We live in a stressful culture and anti-anxiety medications seem to proliferate society like candy on Trick or Treat night. We don't know too much about Gene Reynolds background or genetic make-up, but we read that he is essentially a distraught, demure, introverted man near the end of his rope from the challenges of life. When confronted by some of the vilest, despicable representations of humanity, we expect Gene to get squashed. It is my hope readers were as surprised as the gang of prison thugs when the tables were turned! *Over the Edge* also creates an interesting moral conundrum, for as we root for the consummate protagonist empathetic-underdog to survive in the face of unbridled evil, he slowly evolves into an even more terrifying force of evil. Hope you enjoyed this bloody little mess.

Patrick James Ryan

Spider:

I think every horror writer has a fascination with insects, especially spiders. They're creepy. They have fangs. They bite and release poison. They have multiple legs and cocoon their prey for later meals. What is there not to be afraid of with spiders? A ton of movies have used spiders for fright effects over the years, and horror fiction is loaded with spider stories. There is nothing tremendously original here. Classic formula of spider chemical exposure from corporate toxic waste in rural middle America. Mutated spider meets All-American family and all hell breaks loose. Baseball, apple pie and Chevrolet quickly morph into terror in this simple story of creepy, crawly things run amuck! And yes, I know the pregnancy and birth scene are disgusting. That's why we call it horror! Hope you did not itch too much reading this one.

Puzzles:

The character in *Puzzles* is an arrogant, obnoxious ass! And that is exactly how I wanted him to come across. The story was a bit of an experiment, taking a person with "off-the-chart-intellect," coupled with psychosis and told in the first person. Typically a tough formula to pull off. Not sure I got to where I wanted to go with this little experiment, but at the very least it was fun writing through the lens of a big IQ and throwing around some big vocabulary. All of us have various puzzle pieces that comprise our lives and represent a picture of who we are. Obviously, this intellectual loon has a few missing pieces! I was striving to create a complete absence of empathy, despite the brutal abuse during his upbringing.

Creating lack of empathy in a main character is usually story-suicide, hence this being an experiment. I was also trying to create just enough reader-curiosity that it would compel continued turning of the pages to see the ultimate end of his macabre journey. In that light I hope I succeeded and you stayed with this one!

The Lonely Deaths of Booker and Chance:

Great White Sharks have fascinated us ever since the hugely successful novel *Jaws* by Peter Benchley and the all-time classic movie by Steven Spielberg. *Jaws* was an unrivaled cultural phenomenon in the mid 1970's and its success launched a cavalcade of shark novels and movies still prominent today! *Jaws* had an enormous influence on me and I consider both the book and movie American classics! *JAWS* seems to be on TV at least once a month, forty years after it hit the theaters. It is just as riveting now as it was then. *The Lonely Deaths of Booker and Chance* is an obvious nod of the head to the great works by Benchley and Spielberg, and their profound influence in this particular niche of the genre. I also thought it might be interesting to attempt to create linkage between the real-life shark attacks off the coast of the Jersey Shore in 1916 and the tragic events surrounding the sinking of the *U.S.S. Indianapolis* during World War II. I hesitated though, because the real-life events of the *Indianapolis* were horrific and I know I will be accused of exploiting a tragic event. However, many current readers of the genre are young and many have probably never even heard of the events of the *Indianapolis*, so if I am able to craft a tale that leads readers to research, honor and pay homage to the victims of the Indianapolis, then I am willing to take the heat!!

Booker and Chance are fictitious individuals. Any resemblance to anyone who truly served on the Indianapolis is merely coincidence. For those of you who are younger readers and have not yet had exposure to much history on World War II, pick up a book on the Indianapolis and appreciate the horrific trauma and sacrifice the real men on that ship went through to help fight tyranny. The ending of this story leaves no doubt about my fictitious linkage to a far greater work of fiction, and I hope I paid subtle homage appropriately, as well as to the real life victims of the Jersey Shore attacks and the many honorable men lost to sharks in the Pacific Ocean back in 1945.

The Jupiter Chronicles:

I love science fiction because it often intersects the same path as horror, especially in the classic alien movies, which are personal favorites. *The Jupiter Chronicles* is geared to address the famous question, "What else is out there in that big universe?" Deep in the dark recesses of the human mind, a nagging thought lingers: What if there is intelligent life outside of our realm that has greater capacity to dominate than us? *The Jupiter Chronicles* is a short little yarn designed to tug at that basic fear with a surprise ending.

Hitchin'a Ride:

How many stories and movies have we all read or watched describing the perils of hitchhiking? Well, here's another one! Young guy with a slight punk veneer experiences some predictable car trouble.

Helpful older, seemingly harmless man offers assistance. Who is the victim and who is the predator here? As the story evolves, we see that things are not as they appear. This one has several twists and does not end well for the self-absorbed young man. Be careful who you hitch a ride from. It might just be ole' Bub with a trick or two up his sleeve!

The Bunker:

The Bunker is the longest, and probably the most complex, story in this collection. It is also the second story in the collection where World War II serves as a back drop. Many historians have theorized ties between Adolph Hitler and demonic possession. No figure in the twentieth century up to modern times achieved such a level of dominant influence over a society like Hitler. How did a lowly corporal rise to lead and mesmerize an entire country and impact the world for generations without some kind of higher power? If one buys into this argument, wouldn't it be logical that emissaries of Hell would be sent to assist one, who has found so much favor with the Devil? *The Bunker* takes a deep dive into this very premise against the big picture of the Normandy invasion by the Allies against the Germans. Is it possible that some of the most heinous acts in history were demon-driven or inspired? Makes one think, doesn't it? This one had non-stop action with a bloody conclusion and rather troubling epilogue intended to rattle my faithful reader. Hope you enjoyed it!

The Ripper Returns:

No single serial killer has inspired as much scrutiny and attention as Jack the Ripper, and no single serial killer conjures up almost mythological fear and loathing. I know many books and movies have been done on good old Jack many times before, but I had to do it with my own little fictitious twist on who Jack was, and what happened to him. It was pretty cool weaving historical fact with my made-up stuff! Like the antagonist in *The Bunker*, Jack is not a mere human in *The Ripper Returns*. Hence in my made-up prose, the reason his identity was never been conclusively proven and remains a mystery to this day!

Ma's Eats:

This one was sheer, utter fun to write. From the hillbilly slang vocabulary to multiple influences, including such horror film classics like *The Texas Chainsaw Massacre, Wrong Turn, The Hills Have Eyes, Parents,* and many more. I was striving to create a semblance of normalcy with Ma Lubbock and her kids, portraying outsiders as the real villains and threats to everyday life. I also enjoy many of the food shows on television, and have used many of the good recipes at home with the family from a variety of shows. However, we seem to be a food-obsessed society, so my cannibalistic twist in this story was to turn the tables on an overzealous TV producer, who has no clue about the nefarious origin of the food recipes, and has vastly underestimated the illiterate potential clients he thinks he can manipulate and dominate for profit. The matter-of-fact approach to animal slaughter initially was to lead the reader into thinking the family truly used cows, chickens, pigs and other animals for the recipes. I am sure savvy readers somewhat figured out, or at least suspected, what was really going on, but I took my time introducing it to build some suspense. Nothing fancy here. Just another one of the many families of cannibals in horror land!! LOL!!

---- Patrick James Ryan ---
July 2019

Patrick James Ryan

About the Author

Patrick James Ryan grew up in Columbus, Ohio and started writing after graduating from college with a Bachelor's Degree in Communications and Marketing. After marrying Molly and living vicariously through the sports and activities of their children - Colleen, Michael and Patrick - while balancing work in the financial services industry, Patrick reignited his writing passion in earnest, cranking out his first story collection in a little over a year while working on two novels and a second short story collection at present. An avid sports and music fan, Patrick enjoys Football, Basketball, Baseball, The Beatles, Led Zeppelin and hard rock. In addition to writing, Patrick is a voracious reader, taking in an eclectic swath of fiction and non-fiction across many genres, with horror being a favorite. A practitioner of martial arts for over 25 years, he holds a second-degree black belt and is a huge fan of Bruce Lee. His first book, a collection of macabre stories entitled *Blood Verse* launched his professional writing career to much acclaim, followed by *The Night It Got Out,* his first full-length novel, and *The Maggots Underneath the Porch*, all published by Black Bed Sheet Books. You can also find *Blood Prose,* the poems taken from *Blood Verse* (with a few thrilling extras added) in a separate volume published by Deadman's Tome.

Look for us wherever books are sold.

If you thought *this book* was cool, check out these other titles from the #1 source for the best in independent horror fiction,

BLACK BED SHEET

www.blackbedsheetbooks.com

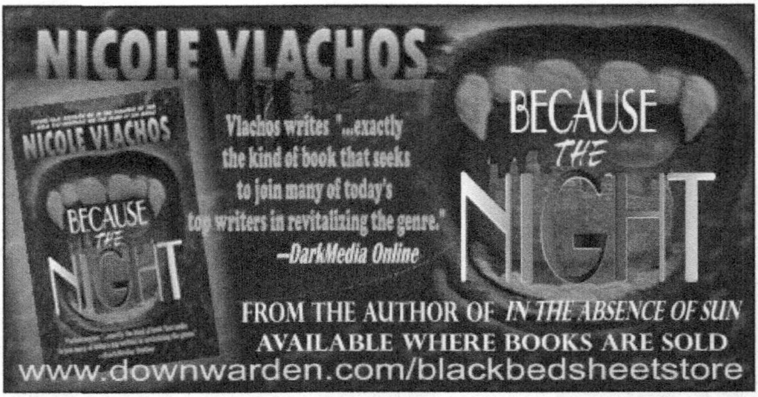

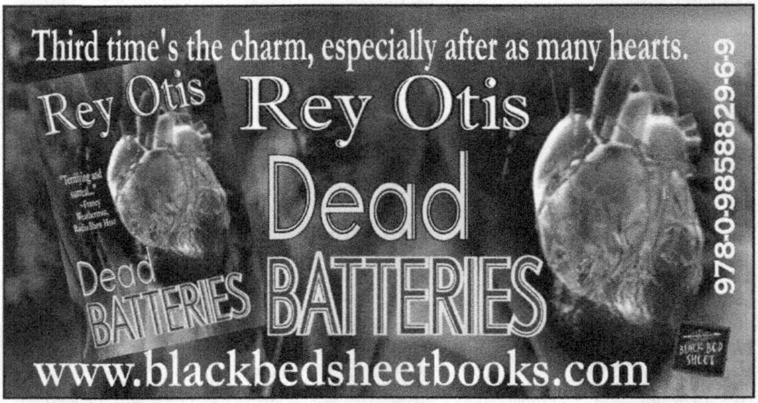

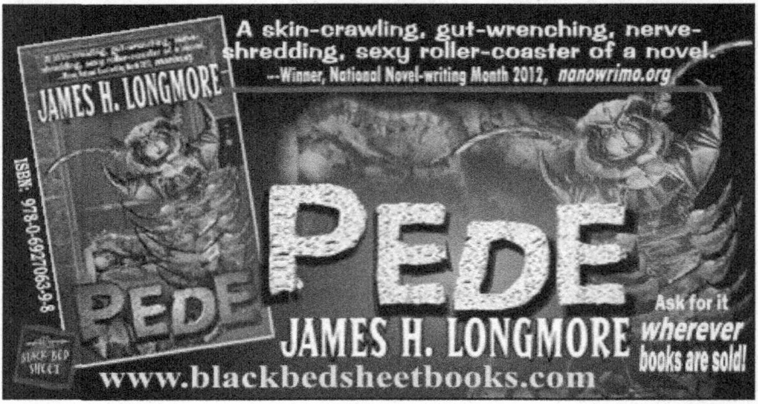

www.blackbedsheetbooks.com

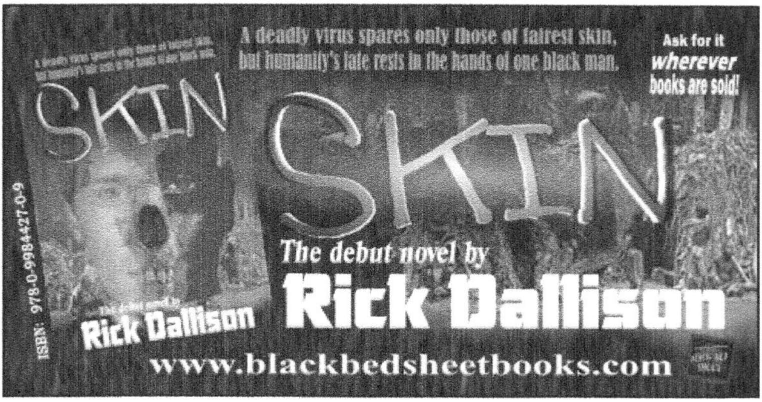

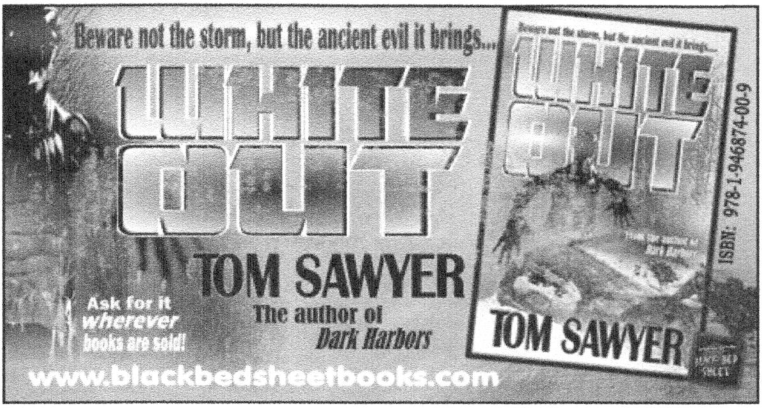

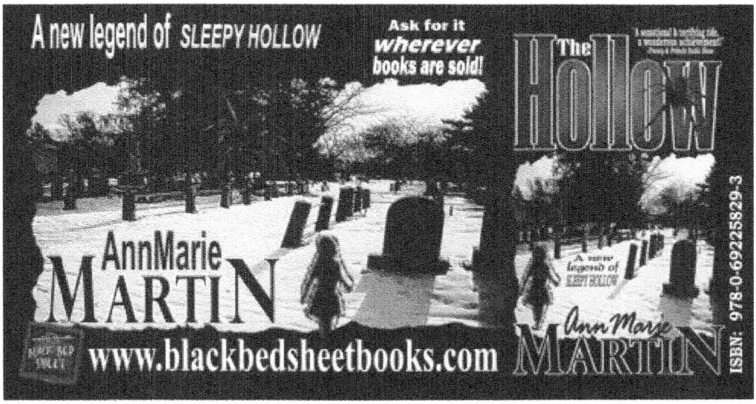

Made in United States
Orlando, FL
02 May 2023